P9-CNI-130

TABOR EVANS

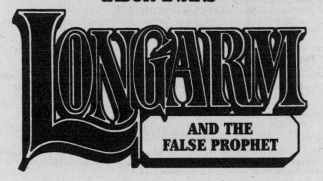

AND THE
FALSE PROPHET

J

JOVE BOOKS, NEW YORK

THE BERKLEY PUBLISHING GROUP
Published by the Penguin Group
Penguin Group (USA) Inc.
375 Hudson Street, New York, New York 10014, USA
Penguin Group (Canada), 90 Eglinton Avenue East, Suite 700, Toronto, Ontario M4P 2Y3, Canada
(a division of Pearson Penguin Canada Inc.)
Penguin Books Ltd., 80 Strand, London WC2R 0RL, England
Penguin Group Ireland, 25 St. Stephen's Green, Dublin 2, Ireland (a division of Penguin Books Ltd.)
Penguin Group (Australia), 250 Camberwell Road, Camberwell, Victoria 3124, Australia
(a division of Pearson Australia Group Pty. Ltd.)
Penguin Books India Pvt. Ltd., 11 Community Centre, Panchsheel Park, New Delhi—110 017, India
Penguin Group (NZ), Cnr. Airborne and Rosedale Roads, Albany, Auckland 1310, New Zealand
(a division of Pearson New Zealand Ltd.)
Penguin Books (South Africa) (Pty.) Ltd., 24 Sturdee Avenue, Rosebank, Johannesburg 2196,
South Africa

Penguin Books Ltd., Registered Offices: 80 Strand, London WC2R 0RL, England

This is a work of fiction. Names, characters, places, and incidents either are the product of the author's imagination or are used fictitiously, and any resemblance to actual persons, living or dead, business establishments, events, or locales is entirely coincidental.

LONGARM AND THE FALSE PROPHET

A Jove Book / published by arrangement with the author

PRINTING HISTORY
Jove edition / June 2006

Copyright © 2006 by The Berkley Publishing Group

All rights reserved.
No part of this book may be reproduced, scanned, or distributed in any printed or electronic form without permission. Please do not participate in or encourage piracy of copyrighted materials in violation of the author's rights. Purchase only authorized editions.
For information, address: The Berkley Publishing Group,
a division of Penguin Group (USA) Inc.,
375 Hudson Street, New York, New York 10014.

ISBN: 0-515-14144-5

JOVE®
Jove Books are published by The Berkley Publishing Group,
a division of Penguin Group (USA) Inc.,
375 Hudson Street, New York, New York 10014.
JOVE is a registered trademark of Penguin Group (USA) Inc.
The "J" design is a trademark belonging to Penguin Group (USA) Inc.

PRINTED IN THE UNITED STATES OF AMERICA

10 9 8 7 6 5 4 3 2 1

If you purchased this book without a cover, you should be aware that this book is stolen property. It was reported as "unsold and destroyed" to the publisher, and neither the author nor the publisher has received any payment for this "stripped book."

DON'T MISS A YEAR OF

SLOCUM GIANT

BY

JAKE LOGAN

SLOCUM GIANT 2003:

THE GUNMAN AND THE GREENHORN

0-515-13639-5

SLOCUM GIANT 2004:

SLOCUM IN THE SECRET SERVICE

0-515-13811-8

SLOCUM GIANT 2005:

SLOCUM AND THE LARCENOUS LADY

0-515-14009-0

AVAILABLE WHEREVER BOOKS ARE SOLD OR AT PENGUIN.COM

B900

J. R. ROBERTS

THE GUNSMITH

THE GUNSMITH #268: BIG-SKY BANDITS	0-515-13717-0
THE GUNSMITH #269: THE HANGING TREE	0-515-13735-9
THE GUNSMITH #270: THE BIG FORK GAME	0-515-13752-9
THE GUNSMITH #271: IN FOR A POUND	0-515-13775-8
THE GUNSMITH #272: DEAD-END PASS	0-515-13796-0
THE GUNSMITH #273: TRICKS OF THE TRADE	0-515-13814-2
THE GUNSMITH #274: GUILTY AS CHARGED	0-515-13837-1
THE GUNSMITH #276: THE CANADIAN JOB	0-515-13860-6
THE GUNSMITH #277: ROLLING THUNDER	0-515-13878-9
THE GUNSMITH #278: THE HANGING JUDGE	0-515-13889-4
THE GUNSMITH #279: DEATH IN DENVER	0-515-13901-7
THE GUNSMITH #280: THE RECKONING	0-515-13935-1
THE GUNSMITH #281: RING OF FIRE	0-515-13945-9
THE GUNSMITH #282: THE LAST RIDE	0-515-13957-2
THE GUNSMITH #283: RIDING THE WHIRLWIND	0-515-13967-X
THE GUNSMITH #284: SCORPION'S TALE	0-515-13988-2
THE GUNSMITH #285: INNOCENT BLOOD	0-515-14012-0
THE GUNSMITH #286: THE GHOST OF GOLIAD	0-515-14020-1
THE GUNSMITH #287: THE REAPERS	0-515-14031-7
THE GUNSMITH #288: THE DEADLY AND THE DIVINE	0-515-14044-9
THE GUNSMITH #289: AMAZON GOLD	0-515-14056-2
THE GUNSMITH #290: THE GRAND PRIZE	0-515-14070-8
THE GUNSMITH #291: GUNMAN'S CROSSING	0-515-14092-9
THE GUNSMITH #292: ALIVE OR NOTHING	0-515-14123-2
THE GUNSMITH #293: THE ROAD TO HELL	0-515-14131-3

Available wherever books are sold or at
penguin.com

(Ad # B11B)

AMBUSHED?

The assassin whirled. Whether the killer heard him, smelled him, or just somehow sensed he was there, Longarm did not know. Whatever the reason, there was a huff of breath like a gasp in the night.

The knife flashed, seeking Longarm's belly to dump his guts onto the floor.

Instinctively, he darted backward, sucking his stomach in tight while he struck down with the clubbed revolver.

Steel met flesh, and he heard the dull, ugly sound of snapping bone.

The killer cried out, and the knife clattered harmlessly onto the floor. Longarm lunged forward and wrapped his arms around the kicking, squirming, sobbing assassin.

The killer was . . . the killer was a girl.

DON'T MISS THESE
ALL-ACTION WESTERN SERIES
FROM THE BERKLEY PUBLISHING GROUP

THE GUNSMITH by J. R. Roberts

Clint Adams was a legend among lawmen, outlaws, and ladies. They called him . . . the Gunsmith.

LONGARM by Tabor Evans

The popular long-running series about Deputy U.S. Marshal Long—his life, his loves, his fight for justice.

SLOCUM by Jake Logan

Today's longest-running action Western. John Slocum rides a deadly trail of hot blood and cold steel.

BUSHWHACKERS by B. J. Lanagan

An action-packed series by the creators of Longarm! The rousing adventures of the most brutal gang of cutthroats ever assembled—Quantrill's Raiders.

DIAMONDBACK by Guy Brewer

Dex Yancey is Diamondback, a Southern gentleman turned con man when his brother cheats him out of the family fortune. Ladies love him. Gamblers hate him. But nobody pulls one over on Dex . . .

WILDGUN by Jack Hanson

The blazing adventures of mountain man Will Barlow—from the creators of Longarm!

TEXAS TRACKER by Tom Calhoun

Meet J.T. Law: the most relentless—and dangerous—manhunter in all Texas. Where sheriffs and posses fail, he's the best man to bring in the most vicious outlaws—for a price.

Chapter 1

"I like you, Longarm. I surely do." United States Marshal Billy Vail leaned back in his chair and smiled. It was the sort of smile, Longarm thought, that a coyote might smile. If coyotes could smile. It sort of gave the impression that Billy was about to pounce on a particularly juicy rabbit. Longarm had to conclude that he was the rabbit.

"Well I like you too, Boss." Longarm tried to smile back at his oh, so innocent-looking employer. He was not sure that he brought it off, though.

"I like you so much, in fact, that for a change you are going to receive an assignment that will be easy. A real snap for you."

"Billy, you're makin' me awful nervous here."

"No, I mean it. This one will be dead easy. Why, you don't even have to do anything. Hardly. No arrests to make. No warrants to serve. Nothing like that. You just need to take a look at something, then come back and make out a report on it. That's all." Billy's smile broadened. It wasn't so much a coyote's smile now, Longarm thought. A wolf maybe. Or a snake.

1

"That, uh . . . I appreciate that. I surely do." Longarm wondered if it was too late to claim he was sick. Or something.

The two men were in Billy Vail's office inside the imposing Federal Building next to the U.S. Mint on Denver's Grant Street where Longarm had hoped to have an easy day of it. But if Billy claimed this would be easy, then Longarm had good reason for concern. Billy never handed the easy ones to his top deputy, which Longarm happened to be.

Longarm fidgeted for a moment, reached inside his tweed coat for a cheroot, pulled his hand back out without one. He was trying to quit and was so serious about it this time that he did not have any cigars on him. Not the slim, wicked little cheroots that he favored nor the long panatelas that he had sent to him by mail from a tobacco shop in St. Louis.

"Are you all right, Custis?"

"Yeah, Boss. Sure thing."

"You look a little peaked. Are you feeling all right?"

"Just fine, thanks." Inwardly he winced. He'd had his chance and hadn't taken it. Dammit.

Custis Long was Marshal Vail's most effective deputy. He could take on wild horses, gangs of desperados, stampeding buffalo, or fallen women without turning a hair. But Billy Vail, dammit, was commencing to worry him.

"Just look at something, then come back an' tell you about it, is that right?"

"Pretty much so, yes. Except I am not the one who wants to know. The Secretary of the Interior has asked to borrow your services."

"The Secre . . . Billy, I don't even know who the sonuvabitch is. Why would he be wantin' me?"

"I misspoke. It is not the Secretary himself who re-

2

quested your help. Rather it was one of his assistants. Or a deputy to an assistant. Some such title as that."

"And would I know this fella?" Longarm asked.

"I doubt it," Billy admitted.

"Then why . . . ?"

"You are on record somewhere in the files they keep in Washington, Longarm, as having successfully dealt with a war chief named Many Thumbs. Now someone back there wants your services again. Since you are, um, already on friendly terms with the man."

"Billy, I would not say me an' him was friendly. Not damn likely. The last time I seen him he swore he was gonna take my hair. And other parts too. I believed him. He woulda tried it if his papa hadn't stepped in an' stopped me from killing him."

"Perhaps the person back in Washington didn't read that part of the file."

"Well, they shoulda."

"Longarm, my friend, you are old enough to know better than to expect common sense from a Washington bureaucrat."

"But jeez, Billy . . ."

"Now Longarm, I told you this assignment will be easy, and it will. All you have to do is look at something. A situation, so to speak. And report back on it." There was that smile again. "Why, you probably won't ever see Many Thumbs at all. Not in person."

"Uh-huh. An' I believe everything you tell me, Boss. Sure I do."

"Yes, well, be that as it may." Billy leaned forward and put his elbows on his desk. "Be that as it may, Deputy Long, your assignment really is a simple one. There is a religious movement that seems to be gaining followers among Many Thumbs' band, and . . ."

3

"This isn't some more of that Ghost Dance shit, is it, Billy, because everybody knows . . ."

"This has nothing to do with Ghost Dancing, Longarm. It might even be a Christian missionary movement. We, that is to say, the government does not know."

"How the hell could the Indian Bureau not know even that little bit, Billy? That don't make sense."

"I did not say that it made sense, Longarm. I said they want you to find out more about it."

"What about the Indian agent for whatever reservation Many Thumbs is on nowadays?"

"Yes, well, um, that seems to be part of the problem."

"Many Thumbs has gone an' jumped the reservation. Is that what you're telling me, Billy?"

"Uh, not exactly. But something along those lines. More or less."

"Getting the tribes t' go back where they belong is the Army's job, Billy, not mine."

"Except in this case, Custis, the job does seem to fall to you." There was that damn smile again. "Because of your past relationship with Many Thumbs."

"Dammit, Billy, d'you know why that son of a bitch is named that?"

"Not really, no."

"It's because he has a necklace made outa the thumb bones . . . from the right hands only . . . of all the people he's killed over the years. He started collecting them when he was just a kid. His camp was hit by raiders from some other tribe, I dunno which. One of 'em came into his lodge—Many Thumbs was eight, ten years old or somethin' like that at the time—an' tried to grab his sister. Many Thumbs whacked the guy over the head. Knocked this fella silly, I guess. The kid grabbed his mama's skinning knife off a mat an' took a swipe at the

4

raider. The raider, he tried to duck, but he was slow. The knife took off his thumb. While he was hollering about that, Many Thumbs stabbed him an' did the job proper this time. But he thought that thumb laying there on the ground was some kinda omen or something.

"Ever since then he's been collecting the damn things. It's grisly I tell you, Billy. I mean, he don't even boil the meat off the thumbs before he adds them to his string. Son of a bitch smells like rotten meat an' those putrefied, half-rotted thumbs look like hell too. He ain't pleasant to be around, I can tell you that."

"All current reports suggest that he is a changed man now, Longarm. Many Thumbs is regarded by his people as a great leader these days and one who wants peace with us whites."

"Peace? Shit. That'll be the damn day."

"Yes, well, that is one of the things you are to report back on."

Longarm scowled. But an assignment was an assignment and he did not want the boss to think he was becoming a shirker. "So where are Many Thumbs an' his band, Billy?"

"Yes, um, that is another thing you are to report back on, Longarm. No one seems to know for sure just where his people are at the moment."

"Oh, Lordy, ain't this gonna be fun."

Longarm stood, a tall, lean man wearing a brown tweed coat and brown corduroy trousers, brown vest with a gold chain extending from pocket to pocket, flat-crowned brown Stetson hat, calf-high black cavalry boots, and a black gunbelt rigged for a cross-draw so he could reach the big Colt .44 with either hand if need be.

He had brown hair, a sweeping handlebar mustache, and warm brown eyes that could turn to granite without warning if he were crossed. His features were weathered and craggy and his physique powerful. He was the sort of man other men instinctively liked. And women just as instinctively wanted.

"You can draw expense vouchers and whatever else you might need, Longarm. See Henry on your way out." Henry was the marshal's secretary, clerk, and chief assistant all rolled into one very efficient package.

"There's times, Boss, when I wish you didn't like me s' damn much," Longarm moaned.

"This is going to be easy, Custis." The coyote smile flashed again. "Trust me."

Chapter 2

This was the moment of truth. The crux of his entire plan. If he wavered now, all he had done so far would come crashing down. But if he did not, it could be disaster. Misery. Pain. Torment. Oh, Lordy, what the *hell* was he to do?

Longarm stood staring down at the many-colored carpetbag that lay open on the foot of the narrow bed in his rented room. For the most part, packing to travel was dead easy. He'd been doing it so often and so long that he scarcely had to think about it any longer, and in fact kept his bag packed and ready to pick up and walk out the door.

Except, that is, for a few last-minute items.

And now . . . now he had to decide. Sink or swim. Make or break. Live or . . . uh, perhaps not that serious. But almost.

Now he had to decide if he should take his usual supply of cheroots and wonderfully mild panatelas.

If he took them, he was pretty sure he would end up smoking them.

But if he did not take any smokes, he could end up in

the middle of some dark and lonely night, hunkered beside the cold dead ashes of a campfire, desperately craving, trembling, quivering, spewing gibberish and fluttering his lips.

The very thought was enough to drive a stake of fear through his chest to pierce his heart.

That stake, he thought, was shaped curiously like a cigar.

What the hell was he, though, a man or a mouse? He could beat this thing. Of course he could.

But the assignment.

The assignment came first. Before any personal considerations, the assignment reigned. Always.

And he would be dealing with Indians up there, wouldn't he? Indians expect visitors to deliver a little present or two, don't they? Whether he encountered Many Thumbs himself or some other leader of power and substance, Longarm was sure to need the cooperation of that person.

Having some cigars on hand would make it far easier. For the sake of the assignment only, of course.

And he could stay away from the cigars even if he did have some in his bag. He was sure that he could. Really.

Longarm opened the treasured cedarwood box that his Hernandez y Hernandez panatelas came in and selected a handful, carefully wrapped them inside some clean underwear, and deposited them tenderly in the middle of his bag. He did the same—perhaps a little less reverently— with a double handful of cheroots. Those he tucked in one end of the bag where they could be easily reached.

Once he had done those things, he was ready to close the bag and walk out the door.

Except—he pulled the railroad-quality Ingersol watch

from his vest pocket to check the time—except he was not yet due at the station for the train north.

And come to think of it, the connection he wanted would not be available until tomorrow morning anyway.

So what was a fellow to do but pass a few hours in leisure until then, eh?

Longarm went downstairs and looked for a hack—like cops the damn things were never around when you needed one—then started walking toward the golden dome of the State Capitol Building gleaming in the distance.

Not that he was going to the Capitol, however. It was just that his favorite watering hole lay in that direction. And a certain young lady who was sure to regret his departure on assignment.

It would be only kind, he felt, to give her an opportunity to assuage the pain of parting.

And she was just the girl to make that sort of pain go away. Yessir, she was for a fact.

"Oh, baby, uh . . . uh . . . uh . . . uh . . ." That was the one thing about Elise that he didn't much care for. She had the habit of grunting into his ear every time he thrusted into her, and the harder he pumped the louder she got. He supposed it should be flattering, taken as a sign that she was enjoying what he had to give her. But dammit, it was distracting.

"Oh . . . oh . . . oh. . . ." She began clawing his back and shoulders, a sure sign she was about to reach one of her climaxes. Longarm braced himself. Sure enough, a few seconds later he felt her body stiffen. Elise arched her back and screeched. Damn near busted his eardrum on that side. She shuddered. She convulsed. She hooked her feet behind his butt and tried to pull him in hips and all.

A moment after that, she went limp. Completely. As in the next thing to passing out on him. Which, in fact, she sometimes did.

Come to think of it . . .

Longarm pulled back a few inches and took a look. Yup. No doubt about it. She was gone. Out cold.

He smiled a little—after all, a girl passing out when she made it was about as sincere a form of flattery as a fellow could ask—and gently withdrew, rolling off her to lie close and warm by her side to wait for her to come around again. These little episodes generally didn't last longer than half a minute or so.

Presently, the girl woke up. Woke up smiling. She stretched, catlike and content, and moved onto her side so she could kiss him.

"Nice," she murmured.

"Nice," Longarm agreed.

"But you didn't make it."

"No. Not yet."

Her smile became wider. "I think we can take care of that."

"I was kinda hoping that you could," he told her with a grin.

"May I ask for a favor, dear?"

"You can ask anything, pretty girl." Pretty girl. And so she was. Elise was an actress, not a headliner but a chorus girl. Blond and small, with ringlets of golden hair and knockers like watermelons, she had a cherubic face that made her look like a kid in her teens even though she was in her late twenties. She sang a little, danced a little, played the part of an ingénue when one was needed. She also liked to fuck. And Longarm liked her. Yes indeed she could ask for a favor. It remained to be seen whether he could grant the request, though.

"You know about the rhythm method of not getting a girl knocked up?"

"I've heard of it, sure," he said.

"Well, I don't know if that stuff works, but I'm supposed to be what you call fertile right about now."

Longarm's eyebrows went up.

"Don't get worried. I don't want you to give me a kid. Just the opposite. I don't want to get knocked up, dear. Not even by you."

He said nothing, but the truth was that her comment was a relief. Fatherhood was not something he needed right now.

"So I was hoping, sweetie, that you would let me suck you off." She began to nibble on his chest. His right nipple was exceptionally sensitive this evening, and Elise seemed to know that. She licked and sucked it while her fingers were busy with his cock and his balls. "Let me take your juice in my mouth. I can't get pregnant that way. Would you do that for me, dear? Please?"

Longarm smiled. And very gently pushed the top of her pretty head down toward an erection that was so hard now that he could have driven nails with it.

Elise licked her way down to his crotch. Her fingers roamed deeper, and she lightly scraped one fingernail over the tight pucker of his asshole.

She buried her face in his middle and sucked his balls, burrowed lower and licked his asshole for a while. Longarm damn near came that way. The girl definitely knew how to please a man.

She licked her way up again, running her tongue up his shaft, then circling around and around the glans before finally she opened her mouth and took him into the wet heat of it.

Longarm shivered. Damn!

She released him for a moment while she looked up and grinned. "Are you in a hurry?"

Longarm shook his head.

"Good." Elise dipped her pretty face to him again and took him deep.

Longarm lay back and let the girl have her way with him.

Chapter 3

There was no quick or easy way to get up into the north of Montana where Many Thumbs had been and might still be. Longarm could have taken a train far to the east and then a steamer up the Missouri. That would put him fairly close. But it was a helluva distance out of the way and sure to be slow.

He settled instead for taking the train to Cheyenne and traveling overland from there. The old Virginia City gold fields were largely played out so there was little traffic going in that direction now, but there was plenty of traffic going to Deadwood and Lead in Dakota Territory. Longarm figured he could take a coach to Deadwood, then hire a horse to get him across to the Missouri, where hopefully he would be able to catch a boat for a quick passage to the upper limits of navigation, then fork a horse again for the last part of the journey.

All of this just to sit back and look at something that might or might not be a problem.

Government, Longarm thought with a weary shake of his head every time he thought about it. Damned government! They didn't know what they were doing, but they were bound and determined to do it anyway.

Still, a job was a job. And it was good to get away from the smoky environs of busy Denver. It was a funny thing about that. Longarm loved the smell of smoke. Generally, that is.

When he was away from the city, the two things that smelled the best to him were the smoke of a cozy fire and coffee on the boil. Either of those was calculated to give a little bump of happiness to his heartbeat, and it did not really matter if the smoke came off a campfire or out of a chimney. It was a good scent, clean and pleasant.

But the smoke from a thousand coal-fed fires like you find in a big city, Denver or any other, was a stench in his nostrils. Morning, night, or in between, it lies over top of the city like a hair blanket, creating itches there is no way to scratch.

Cheyenne was not quite so bad, being a much smaller community than bustling Denver. And in Cheyenne the wind blows.

Longarm stepped down onto the platform at the depot in Cheyenne and grabbed his hat. Yup, he thought. In Cheyenne the wind blows. All the damn time.

One thing or another, he thought with a rueful grin. You gotta put up with some shit in life and there is just no getting away from it.

He slung his old McClellan ball-breaker over his shoulder—the Army-surplus saddle was a bitch to ride, but it was easy on a horse's back—tucked the Winchester and scabbard under his arm, and picked up the carpetbag with his other hand. It was a good thing he only had a few blocks to go to reach his favorite little rooming house in the city.

He hiked the distance without dropping anything,

cussing pretty much every step of the way because he hadn't thought to light a cigar before he got himself all loaded down like this and he did not want to stop now and then have to start all over. He was pleased when he finally reached the front porch of Mrs. Benson's and dumped everything beside one of the cane-bottom rocking chairs sitting there. He immediately grabbed a cheroot and match and got the two of them acquainted.

"Now that's better," he mumbled aloud as he drew that first sweet puff deep into his lungs.

He heard the creak of a spring and the squeal of hinges as the front door opened. A heavyset man with a fringe of gray hair set halolike around a bald dome peered out. "Oh. Thought I heard someone out here. What d'you want, mister?"

"I'm looking for Mrs. Benson," Longarm said. "I'll be needing a room for the night."

"The old lady's dead," the bald man said bluntly.

"No. Damn!" Longarm unconsciously swept his hat off out of respect for the lady. "What happened?"

"All I know is she died. I own the place now. Bought it from her son."

"Her son is in Australia digging for gold," Longarm said.

The fellow nodded. "That's right, he is. That's where I was too until I decided I didn't want to see an ocean no more. Him and me met in a pub. Time I sobered up, I had the deed to this here place and he had all my brass."

"What about the daughter?"

The bald man shrugged. "She left. I told her she could stay on as hired help, but she got all huffy and walked out. I haven't seen her since."

"That's a shame," Longarm said, without specifying whether he meant Mrs. Benson dying or the girl leaving.

15

"You still want that room?"

"Yeah, I expect so. She always used to give me the room upstairs in the back on this side here."

"Staying long, are you?"

"Only for the one night."

"You can have the room beside the kitchen. It's downstairs. Easy to reach the shitter."

"It's tiny and there's no window," Longarm said.

"It's also the room you can have. Hell, it's only for one night. A bloke can put up with anything for one night. You want that room or don't you?"

Longarm sighed. "Yeah. I suppose so."

"One dollar. In advance. More if you got a horse."

"No horse." Longarm dug into his pockets and produced a dollar. "I'll need a receipt for that."

"I'll write one out. You got breakfast comes with that. No supper. You can find that on your own or eat here for a quarter."

The old lady used to include both breakfast and supper. And she did not charge extra to stable a horse either. Still, the man was entitled. It was his business now.

"Reckon I can find something in town," Longarm told him.

"Suit yourself. You know where the room is. Help yourself." The bald man withdrew from the door without ever bothering to introduce himself. Longarm jammed his cheroot between his teeth and picked up his gear again.

Longarm was in no great rush to return to the boardinghouse. It was a shitty little room that he'd been given, airless with no window, and it smelled of grease because of being jammed up against a very flimsy kitchen wall. He suspected the spot was originally intended to be a pantry and not a bedroom at all, or at best some sort of servant's quarters. Mrs. Benson only pressed it into service as a last resort when everything else was full. And then she always discounted the price.

Still, Longarm kept telling himself, this man had a right to run his own business in his own way. If Custis Long happened not to like it, he was welcome to go somewhere else to sleep. And the truth was that he would have done exactly that and headed downtown to one of the hotels except for having to carry everything if he did so. As saddles went, the McClellan was not particularly heavy, but when combined with a Winchester and carpetbag, it was enough of a load to be a nuisance.

And it was only for one night. Hell, he could put up with anything for only one night, just like the bald man had said.

He had a good supper of baked scrod and jacket potatoes, marveling at the notion that in a railroad town a man could find pretty much anything he wanted, right down to raw oysters that had been shipped on ice and arrived fresh every day or two. He might have had some oysters on the half shell except for the outrageous price. The restaurant wanted seventy-five cents the dozen. A man had to be awfully rich to spend like that. Longarm figured the fish and taters were plenty civilized enough, but he wanted to have himself a fancy meal while he still could. Once he left Cheyenne and the influence of the railroad, things were apt to turn plain in a hurry.

He drew the line at having wine with his dinner, but did indulge in brandy and a panatela before ambling down the street for a friendly game of chance to wile away the remainder of the evening. It was probably approaching midnight before he returned to the boardinghouse and his bleak little room.

He shucked down to his smallclothes and slipped beneath the blanket, expecting to hear nothing but the sound of his own snoring.

Instead, his intended rest was disturbed by a small and persistent mewling sound.

It took Longarm a few minutes to recognize the muted noise. It was that of someone—a woman, he thought—weeping.

Frowning, Longarm sat up on the edge of the narrow, rope-sprung bed and reached for his britches.

Chapter 4

He recognized her from the times he had stayed there before, although he could not recall her name. The serving girl was small, black, perhaps thirty or thereabouts. She was sitting on a pallet laid on the kitchen floor beside the stove. She was softly crying, her thin shoulders shuddering with the depth of her misery. The woman looked up when Longarm came into the room.

She jumped to her feet and reached to a lamp on the table, its wick turned as low as was possible without extinguishing the flame. She twisted the knob to adjust the flame higher, and the room filled with a flood of yellow light.

"Yes, sir. What can I . . . what can I get for you, sir?"

"I don't mean to disturb you," he said, "and there's nothing I need at the moment. I heard you crying. I came to see if there is anything I can do for you."

"Oh, you . . . you be nice, Mr. Long. Miz Benson, she always say how nice a man you are."

"Forgive me please but I've forgotten your name."

"I am Ruby, sir."

"Yes, of course. Now I remember." He didn't, but what the hell. "What is wrong, Ruby? Why are you crying?"

"I don't mean t' bother a fine gentleman such as yourself, sir. You don't fret yourself over the likes of me or Missy Lila."

"Lila Benson?" he asked. "Is she here? I was told she left." Lila was the dead landlady's spinster daughter. Longarm remembered her well enough. Lila was fat and a little soft in the head and had a mustache. But she had a good heart and a wonderful laugh. He'd always suspected Lila had a crush on him. She would be about the same age as Ruby, he thought.

"Miss Lila live over by the railroad tracks," Ruby said.

"What is she doing for a living?"

"She . . . you know . . . she does for men. Sometimes. Most won't be wanting her, but she get by. I slip her food out the back door. She get by," Ruby said.

Longarm sighed. He could just imagine the sort of trade poor, ugly Lila would be able to attract. The mean and the miserly, that would be about it.

"I'm sorry to hear that, Ruby. But what about you? Why are you upset this evening?"

"I just sad, sir. I don't like it here now that Mr. Adam be the boss."

"Perhaps you should leave, Ruby. I know what a good worker you are. I'm sure you could find another job somewhere that you do like."

"Oh, I can't leave here, sir. Mr. Adam say he file the papers on me if I try to leave before I pay everything I owe. He say I go to jail. I can't leave until my debt be clear, sir. Mr. Adam have his lawyer friend explain it to me. Show me the paper. That paper, it all signed and everything. Do he take it to the co'thouse and file it, I be sent to jail for certain sure. So I stay here and do . . . I have to do whatever Mr. Adam want."

"You mean work for him here like you did when Mrs. Benson was alive?"

"That too, sir. That work and . . . other things too."

"What other things, Ruby?"

"You know. Like Miss Lila have to do except only for Mr. Adam and his friends."

"They force you to have sex, Ruby?"

The little woman nodded. She lifted the hem of her apron and scrubbed some of the tear tracks off her face, then wiped her nose.

"Do they hit you?"

"Sometimes. Mr. Adam, he the only one do that, though. The other gentlemen, they not so bad. Mr. Adam like it best when I crying while I . . . while I do him. You know. Get down on my knees and do him. He like that the most."

"Tell me about this debt you owe, Ruby."

"I don't understand it exactly. It all in that paper the lawyer man write down. They try to explain it to me but I'm not so smart, Mr. Long. I don't really know except they have it all down in that paper and I go to jail if Mr. Adam file that paper at the co'thouse."

Longarm stepped forward and touched Ruby on the shoulder. He patted her and gave her an encouraging squeeze. Ruby apparently misunderstood his meaning. She immediately dropped to her knees, her expression frozen.

"No, no, no, dear. That is *not* what I was telling you," he quickly said.

"But . . ."

"Get up, Ruby. You don't have to do that. Not ever

21

again, not unless it is something you decide you want to do for someone. But no one is going to force you to do that—or anything else—ever again."

"Sir?"

Longarm smiled at her. "Tell me more about Mr. Adam and this paper, Ruby. In fact"—he pulled out a chair and sat at the table—"in fact, I would like for you to pour us each a cup of nice cold water. Then I would like you to sit here with me and tell me everything you can remember about your situation and Lila's."

Ruby seemed uncertain, but she was accustomed to obedience. She did what she was told.

Many Thumbs was just going to have to wait for one more day before he and his old "friend" Custis Long became reaquainted. There was something Longarm figured he needed to do here in Cheyenne first.

He had been up late the night before, so he allowed himself the luxury of sleeping in come morning. That was made considerably easier by the fact that with no window in the room there was no intrusion of sunlight to warn him about time. By the time he woke, the other boarders had already finished their breakfasts and gone off to whatever it was they did. Ruby was alone in the kitchen washing the guests' breakfast dishes. The bald man was seated in the parlor with a newspaper open in his lap and a cup of steaming coffee at his elbow.

Longarm looked in on him and nodded a good-morning, but did not bother making conversation with the son of a bitch. After speaking with Ruby, he knew too much about Adam Franzler to be pleasant with him. Instead, Longarm backed out of the parlor entrance and turned back toward the rear of the house.

"Good morning, sir. I saved food for you. Sit there, please."

"Thank you, Ruby." Longarm returned to the chair he had spent several hours on earlier that morning while he'd tried to make sense of Ruby's rather garbled account of the legal claims Franzler said he could place against her.

The small woman poured coffee for him, then produced a platter from the warming oven containing a dozen or more incredibly light and fluffy biscuits. She set a pan of thick gravy in reach and followed that with a small crock of sweet butter, a pot of strawberry jam, and another of honey.

"I can't fry you no bacon or eggs, sir," she apologized. "Only person here gets to eat like that be Mr. Adam."

Longarm smiled at her and winked. "That's all right, Ruby. Biscuits and gravy is my favorite." Especially with a mess of pork chops to accompany them, but he did not mention that lest Ruby start to feel bad about not pleasing him.

He checked the time—it was past nine—and ate quickly. He just wished. . . . Dammit, Ruby was uneducated, and Lila was soft in the head. Franzler was counting on being able to bamboozle both of them.

When he was done, Longarm thanked Ruby and got his hat. He left his saddle and Winchester in the room, however.

"I'll be staying another night," Longarm informed Franzler on his way out. He gave the landlord another dollar.

"I'll have your receipt ready when you return," Franzler told him.

"Good enough." Longarm hurried outside and headed

for the railroad tracks. According to Ruby, LilaBenson was living in a pair of large packing crates that she'd found somewhere and dragged behind the stock pens. Longarm surely did want to have a word with Lila before he made his second visit of the day.

Chapter 5

Sam Jessup looked up from the paperwork on his desk and smiled. "Longarm!" He sounded genuinely pleased. "It's good to see you, old friend. What a nice surprise."

"Hello, Sam." Longarm crossed the Cheyenne police chief's office and extended his hand to the tall, dark-haired man. Chief Jessup was lean and had sun wrinkles at his eyes, but he was losing the deep tan that used to be normal for him. And nowadays he was carefully barbered with the scent of bay rum hanging in the air around him, and his hair was parted in the middle and slicked down with some sort of oil or ointment. Like Billy Vail, though, Sam Jessup was a lawman from the old school. He had ridden the trails and faced the bad ones, and he was the one who was still upright and breathing after those encounters. He took no shit, but he knew how to dish it out. Longarm liked him. So did Billy.

"Sit down, Longarm. Do you have an assignment here? Anything I can help you with?"

"No assignment, Sam. This is something I'm doin' kinda on my own."

Jessup nodded and waited patiently for Longarm to continue.

"Is Harvey still pushing papers for the fat cats, Sam?"

"Show a little respect for your betters, Longarm. But yes, Harvey is still there. In fact he's gotten himself a promotion. He is an assistant to the Attorney General now."

"All the better," Longarm said. Harvey Roberts started out as a deputy when Sam Jessup was undersheriff here, then moved to the city's payroll as a police sergeant when Sam accepted the appointment as chief of police. On his own time Harvey read law until he felt competent to hang out his shingle as a lawyer. He became the city's prosecutor and the last Longarm knew, had left that position to move into a junior position with the territorial government. It seemed that young Harvey was still moving quickly up the ladder. Longarm would not be surprised if someday Harvey Roberts turned up as Attorney General of the United States of America.

Longarm grinned at that thought.

"What are you smirking about?" Sam asked.

When Longarm told him, Sam laughed. "Wouldn't that be a kick in the britches, you working for Harvey."

"It could happen," Longarm said.

"Yes, I expect it could." Sam leaned back and pushed his paperwork aside. "Now tell me why you are asking about Harvey, old friend. And what I can do to help with this thing you are doing on your own."

Longarm pulled out a pair of panatelas and offered one to Sam, then lighted them both and helped himself to a seat in front of Sam's desk. He commenced to talk. And Sam commenced to grin.

When Longarm was done, Sam steepled his fingers

and stared into them for a moment, then said, "There is one thing I would change."

"Tell me," Longarm invited.

"We don't go ourselves. The three of us will wait here and . . . no, even better, the two of us, just you and I, will wait here. We'll send one of my constables to fetch the subject. In fact, I know the very fellow I will give that job. We'll have our little meeting here, then all three walk over to the Capitol Building. Harvey can wait there for his part in the deal. We'll have to have it all worked out ahead of time, of course." Sam chuckled. "Over lunch. You can buy, Longarm. It's about time you make yourself useful around here."

"All right, Sam. I'll buy. But I get t' pick the place then."

"Fair enough." Jessup stood and reached for his hat. "Let's go get Harvey and drag him in on this deal."

Longarm belched. Damn, that had been a good lunch. Fried pork chops, fried potatoes, fried apples . . . if he could have figured out a way to fry the coffee too, the meal would have been perfect.

They knocked at the boardinghouse door. As a paying guest there, Longarm had the right to go on in without announcing himself, but under the circumstances that just wouldn't have seemed right.

"Is Mr. Franzler here?" Longarm asked Ruby when she answered the door.

"Yes, sir. Mr. Adam be in the parlor with his lawyer friend. But he say he not to be disturbed, Mr. Long. Best you come back this afternoon, I think."

"How very convenient," Longarm muttered.

Sam Jessup removed the derby that he had taken to

wearing now that he was a city fellow and stepped inside. "You say the gentleman is in the parlor, miss?"

"Yes, sir. Him and Mr. Benjamin."

Sam frowned in concentration. "Benjamin? I don't remember any lawyer in town named Benjamin."

"Oh, that not his proper name, sir. He is Mr. Benjamin Albright."

"That explains it," Sam said. "I already know Mr. Albright." Sam turned to Longarm and said, "Ben Albright is an inventory clerk for the Union Pacific."

"Oh, no, sir. Mr. Benjamin, he be a lawyer."

Sam took Ruby by the elbow. "I think you might enjoy coming with us, miss. Just stay back out of the way where you won't get hurt."

"Hurt, sir? Why you think I be hurt?"

"I don't think there will be any trouble. But you never know how someone is going to act when he's being carted off to jail."

"Jail, sir? Mr. Benjamin?"

Longarm grinned. "Could be, Ruby. But Franzler is going for sure."

"Involuntary servitude for starters," the chief of police said. "Confiscation of wages. Could be grand theft too depending on whether he can produce a properly recorded deed to this house and witnesses to attest to his purchase of it."

"What it comes down to," Longarm said, "is that unless Franzler can get some witnesses here from Australia mighty sudden, this house is gonna revert back to Lila Benson and you, and Lila will be able to run it like her mama used to."

The colored girl beamed. "You think so, sir?"

"Oh, we're pretty sure of it, Ruby. Pretty sure indeed."

"Adam Franzler will be in the territorial penitentiary

for a good many years by the time we're done with him—"

"Unless he's smart enough to make bail and get the hell out of town," Longarm interrupted, "which would be perfectly all right too."

"—and that skunk of a phony lawyer will at least spend a few days in the city jail," Sam concluded. "I can see to that much myself. As for exactly how long, that will depend on how good a lawyer he can afford to hire."

Longarm laughed. "Unless he wants to step up to the bar and try t' defend himself, that is."

"Now if you would be so good as to show us the way to the parlor, miss, we have a real lawyer . . . and a good one . . . waiting to file charges against these two just as quick as we get them over to the Capitol."

Ruby scurried ahead to show the gentlemen the way. She pointed to the closed door and stepped aside. She was smiling when she did so.

Chapter 6

"Y'know," Longarm mused over a glass of whiskey late that afternoon, "there's times when it feels good t' be a lawman."

Chief of Police Sam Jessup grinned and lifted his own glass toward Longarm in a small salute. "Don't I know what you mean."

"The look on Adam Franzler's face when you snapped those handcuffs on him." Longarm took a pull at the whiskey. It wasn't rye but it was good. "That right there was fine. An' the sound of the steel locking into place. Yessir. Mighty fine."

"Franzler is not a happy boy tonight, I think," Sam said. "But he might as well get used to looking at the world from inside a cell. He's going to be in one for a long time to come."

"It's federal charges that he's facing mostly," Longarm said. "I'll wire Billy tonight. Tomorrow he can alert the U.S. Attorney an' get him to coordinate with Harvey and your territory boys."

"I really don't expect the man to be here for trial," Jessup said. "Harvey is going to recommend bond for him. Something low enough that he can meet it. Not that we are going to actually *tell* him to jump bail and get the hell out of here, mind. But he should get the message. Especially after Harvey goes over all the likely charges and the probable prison sentences. He won't want to face that. He'd be away for years."

"D'you think you and Harvey can get her mama's business put in Lila's name?" Longarm put his feet up on the seat of one of the unused chairs between them in the quiet little saloon where he and Jessup were enjoying their drinks.

"If Franzler jumps bail and runs, it will be no problem at all. We can simply vacate his deed as it being an abandoned property and get a court to pass it to the closest relative. Which would be Lila."

"You figure the court would be, um, friendly t' that idea?"

Jessup smiled. "I can almost guarantee it."

"And if Franzler is fool enough to stay t' stand trial?"

"Oh, I think we could convince him to convey the title. But I'd rather not do that. It would give the charges the appearance of a malicious prosecution. A good lawyer could jump on that and possibly get enough mileage out of it to confuse a juror, and all he would need would be one man to cause a mistrial, maybe even an acquittal. We certainly would not want that."

"Speaking of lawyers. An' folks that pretend t' be lawyers but really ain't . . ."

Jessup shrugged. "Ben Albright is going to get a scare but not much in the way of real punishment. I have him in my jail for tonight. Maybe I can keep him there for another day or two before I haul him in front of the justice of the peace, but he doesn't have much to worry about.

"Once I stand him up in front of the judge, he can expect a stern talking-to but not much else. After all, he personally didn't defraud anyone. Franzler did that. Albright was just helping a buddy. He can claim he thought it was all a joke. A jury could very likely believe that. A lot of people in town know Ben. They will be willing to give him the benefit of the doubt."

Longarm finished his whiskey and motioned for refills for himself and for Sam Jessup too. "I don't have a problem with Albright," he said. "Getting Lila Benson and Ruby safe and taken care of is all I wanted out of it."

"It won't give you any heartburn to see Franzler free and on the run?"

"Not a bit of it," Longarm said. He grinned. "But it sure was good to see him squirm when you snapped those irons on him this afternoon, Sam. Damn but it was."

"Doing good," Jessup said. "That's the biggest reward a lawman can hope to get."

"That an' taking down the sons o' bitches who're up to no good," Longarm agreed.

Sam lifted his newly filled glass to Longarm again and Longarm returned a silent toast of his own. This hadn't been a bad day's work.

Chapter 7

It took Longarm eight days of hard travel to get from Cheyenne to the Army's Camp Converse on the Bright Star Reservation.

Bright Star my ass, Longarm thought as he rode out of the pines and down a slope to the creek bottom where the reservation was located. Whoever had named the place had obviously never seen it. No, to be fair, he realized, they may well have seen it. Before the several bands of Indians arrived.

The location really was pleasant enough, situated as it was in a broad valley with low hills all around and snow-capped mountain peaks in the distance to the east and west. Originally, the valley was probably soft with lush grasses and wildflowers.

Now it was just plain butt-ugly.

Fields of knee-high stumps covered the hillsides in all directions where timber had been harvested for fuel and construction needs. At the east end of the camp the Army detachment was living in low-roofed quarters made of piled sod. Several acres where that sod had been cut were once grass, now turned to mud after the grass had been removed.

Several herds of spotted ponies had overgrazed the grass that remained. There were just too many animals for the available forage, and no one seemed to have either the money or perhaps the inclination to bring in feed from elsewhere.

The Indians—several different bands from several different tribes, all of them thrown together in this place against their will—lived in crudely built log shacks scattered on both sides of the creek that flowed down from the hills to the west and northwest and exited the valley to the southeast.

The Bright Star Reservation had become an ugly boil on the backside of what should have been a perfectly lovely piece of country. It was a damn shame, Longarm thought. He really couldn't blame anyone red, white, or otherwise who did not care to live here.

But then the Great Father's little red children had no choice in the matter.

Little red children! Yeah, right. The fat politicians back East who thought that way had never faced one of those "children" across the sights of a good rifle. The people who were kept bottled up here, put away out of sight and out of mind, were grown men and grown women. There were thieves among them and philanderers and wife-beaters and drunks and pretty much a little bit of everything else too. Just like in any like-sized community of whites.

There were also hard workers and brave warriors and loving husbands who laughed and sang and played with their children. Just like in any like-sized community of whites.

Shit, it was no wonder Many Thumbs had jumped the

reservation. Longarm would rather live as a fugitive in the mountains than as a ward of the government here on the Bright Star Reservation.

But then no one had asked for his opinion on the subject.

And, truth be told, if Many Thumbs wanted to raise some hell—and some hair—it could be tough on an awful lot of folks, red and white, who only wanted to live their lives in peace. Many Thumbs was a son of a bitch when he was on the warpath, killing, raping, and scalping with happy abandon. Longarm had seen his handiwork before. Had heard the crying and helped to bury the bodies that Many Thumbs left behind. He did not want to see that happen again.

He found a path through the weathered stumps where pine trees once grew, and made his way down toward the dreary camp where a squad of infantry was drilling on a muddy flat near a makeshift flagpole. Old Glory hung limp there.

"You there. Corporal. Where can I find the post commander?" Longarm inquired of the noncom who was in charge of the soldiers.

"Squad, halt! At ease." The corporal turned and came jogging over to the horse Longarm had hired back at the Missouri River. "What was that, sir?"

"Your commanding officer, Corporal. Where can I find him?"

The corporal glanced toward the sun, obviously gauging the time of day. It was the middle of the afternoon, probably around two-thirty, Longarm guessed. He did not bother pulling out his watch to check for sure, if only because he did not much give a damn.

"I wouldn't know for sure, mister, but I'd say the lieutenant is most likely, um, in his quarters, sir, and not to be disturbed."

37

"There's a lieutenant in charge here, Corporal?"

"Yes, sir. Lieutenant Haynes, sir."

"Just how large is your contingent?" It had to be damn small, Longarm realized, for a lowly lieutenant to be in overall command of the garrison.

"There's two squads of us, sir. I'm the senior noncommissioned officer. Corporal Brawley has the other squad. They're off cutting wood this afternoon. We kind of take turnabout on that. Is there, uh, anything I can help you with, sir? Until the lieutenant is available, I mean."

"Where are your visiting officer's quarters, Corporal?"

The man removed his kepi and ran a hand through hair that had begun to thin. "I guess that'd be in the lean-to on the side of the headquarters building there, sir. I think there's a cot in there that the officer of the day is supposed to use. Except we got no other officers so me and Tom—Corporal Brawley, I mean—me and him stand duty there when there's need."

Longarm smiled. "Like when there is brass visiting?"

The corporal grinned. "Something like that, sir. Say, you aren't, uh . . ."

"No, I'm no one like that, Corporal. But I will be occupying the lean-to while I'm here." Longarm introduced himself.

"Anything I can do for you, sir, you just let me know. I'll see to it myself. My name is Lassiter, sir. Ed Lassiter. I'll take care of you."

"I'm sure you will, Ed. Now if you could direct me to the Indian agent for this reservation?"

"Oh, we got no agent here, sir. Not no more. He up and quit. That was last winter. Awful bad winters here, sir. Him and his wife couldn't take it. The way I heard it, the lady gave him the choice of stayin' here alone or going out with her alongside." The corporal's grin flashed again. "I'm thinking he made the wrong choice when he left, but who am I t' say?"

Longarm laughed. He stepped down from the horse and extended his hand to Ed Lassiter. The corporal seemed a little surprised, but he returned the gesture. "It's a pleasure t' meet you, sir."

"And mine, Ed."

"Can I take your horse for you, sir? It'd give my boys something to do. Keeping them busy is always a problem around here."

"All right, thank you."

"The lieutenant will be along by and by, sir. He'll come over to headquarters when he's done sc—uh, he'll report there quick as he's available, sir."

"Are those his quarters there, Ed?" Longarm pointed toward one of the very few other log buildings on the tiny post. The enlisted men might make do in sod huts, but an officer would surely want a real building for himself.

"Yes, sir, but like I said . . ."

"Yeah. I know. The lieutenant is"—Longarm smiled—"busy."

"He won't be long, sir. Won't be long at all now."

Longarm glanced around in time to see a slim figure with long hair and bare feet slip outside and quickly around the side of the building.

"Yes, I see what you mean," Longarm said dryly. It seemed the lieutenant enjoyed a little afternoon diversion. Longarm removed his bedroll and the carpetbag that he carried tied behind his cantle, and headed for the headquarters building carrying those along with his Winchester, leaving the horse to Corporal Lassiter and his squad.

Chapter 8

Lieutenant George Haynes was a thin, gangly man with
lank yellow hair that he wore long, either because he was
trying to ape the long-dead Custer or because he was simply lax about getting it cut. It would have made a splendid
scalp for someone like Many Thumbs, Longarm thought
as he was shaking the man's hand.

"Lassiter tells me you are a United States marshal?"

Longarm shook his head. "The marshal is back in
Denver sitting behind a pile o' paperwork. I'm just one of
his deputies."

"Don't tell me we have a criminal in our midst here,
Deputy. The corporal did not tell me what brought you all
the way out here to the ends of the earth."

"That bad, is it?"

"Oh, pay no attention to me, Long. Sometimes I have
visions of scaling the heights. Rank and glitter and all of
that. Then I wake up and look around me. This may surprise you, but we host very few cotillions here."

"It is kinda a small post, ain't it," Longarm sympathized.

"We had a full company to begin with, but these Indi-

ans are thoroughly cowed. We have small bands repre-
senting the castoffs from five different tribes confined
here. I believe there was some concern about them to begin with. Their own tribes considered them to be trouble-
makers. Or they simply did not fit in with the others of
their kind. But since they came here they've caused no
trouble and are not likely to engage in any.

"Things are so peaceful that the War Department si-
phoned off our people until we few brave souls are all
that is left. The regiment is scattered across Idaho, Montana, and the Dakotas with the bulk of my company in the
south of Dakota Territory."

"You say the Indians here are peaceful?" Longarm
asked.

"Oh, yes. Completely."

"Even Many Thumbs, Lieutenant?"

"Especially Many Thumbs, Deputy."

Longarm raised an eyebrow. "Lieutenant, I find that
kinda hard to accept. I knew Many Thumbs before. The
man is a sonuvabitch. Pure meanness on the hoof. Now
you're telling me he's peaceful?"

"Yes, I am, Deputy. The man has found religion."

"He isn't doing that Ghost Dancing shit, is he?"

Haynes laughed. "He has found the true religion,
Long. Many Thumbs has become a devout Christian."

"Damn," Longarm muttered. "Then if that's so, let me
ask you why he broke out an' jumped the reservation."

The lieutenant looked confused. "Wherever did you
hear such a thing as that?"

"Many Thumbs leaving the reservation is why I come
here, Lieutenant. There's folks back East who worry
about him maybe going back to the scalping knife."

"I wish someone had asked me about this. I could have
set them straight without putting you to a lot of bother."

"Hell, I wish they had my own self if this is the truth o' the matter."

"Oh, I can assure you that it is."

"I was told that Many Thumbs jumped the reservation an' took all his people with him. I was told nobody knows where he is or what he is up to."

Haynes shook his head. "If the War Department contacted anyone about this it must have been the battalion commander. He certainly would not know and could not begin to guess. They really should have asked me. But then communication here is what you might call slow. We have no telegraph. We receive mail and supplies and a visit from the paymaster once every two months or so."

"What about the Bureau of Indian Affairs? Corporal Lassiter said the agent assigned here walked out last winter."

"More like early last fall," Haynes said. "He and his wife left immediately after the first snowfall. That would have been in September or thereabouts. Any mail that has come addressed to him has been marked for return to the sender and sent out on the next supply train."

"And Many Thumbs is still on the reservation?" Longarm asked.

"Now I did not exactly say that. I said he has not taken his people and fled the reservation. In fact, he is still on Bright Star land. But not in the vicinity of Camp Converse."

"Lieutenant, I'm confused. Could you lay this out a little plainer?"

"It is fairly simple, Deputy. Last fall we were visited by a preacher. An evangelist, you might call him. The Reverend J. Samuel Dascher. The Reverend Dascher came on a mission of salvation, he and his companions who have also seen the light and converted to the faith.

43

"The reverend asked permission to preach to these Indians. I, of course, granted it. He led them into the wilderness and spoke to them. Some of the men claim he preached to them in their own tongue. I would not know about that. I did not personally hear any of the things he said. But I did personally observe the changes that came over his newfound flock.

"Many Thumbs in particular was taken with him. Until the Reverend Dascher came along, my greatest fear was that Many Thumbs would indeed decide to go back onto the warpath. And with only two squads of infantry here at Converse to oppose him, that could have been a terrible thing. Simply terrible."

"Yes, sir," Longarm affirmed. "I've seen Many Thumbs' handiwork in the past. I hope I won't ever see it again."

"Nor shall you, Deputy. I can assure you of that."

"So where is Many Thumbs now?"

"The Reverend Dascher appointed a core group of Indians . . . his Mighty Men, he calls them . . . and led them and their families into the wilderness again. Still on the Bright Star Reservation, however. He assured me that his intention was not to leave the bounds of the reservation. He merely wanted privacy so he can have these tribal leaders alone. He will indoctrinate them in the lore of his faith and appoint them as his apostles to reach out to other Indians."

"He's gonna make an apostle of *Many Thumbs*?" Longarm asked incredulously.

"That is his intention, yes."

"So I can go back to my boss in Denver an' tell him that this whole thing about a breakout from Bright Star is all just a big mistake an' the government shouldn't bother worryin' about it, is that right?"

"Yes," Haynes said with a wide smile. "That is exactly right."

Longarm whistled softly. "Of all the things I might've imagined to find here, Lieutenant, this would be just about the last damn thing amongst 'em." He shook his head. "Many Thumbs. An apostle. Who the hell woulda ever thought a thing like that."

Haynes cleared his throat and said, "We are rather informal here, Deputy, but I hope you will dine with us this evening. The men eat immediately after retreat. Naturally I would like to have you at my table. That would be about an hour later. I'll send a runner to call you."

"All right, Lieutenant. That'd be fine. Thank you."

Haynes disappeared inside the headquarters building while Longarm ambled around the corner toward the lean-to where he'd put his gear. He would want to break out the panatelas after supper as a thank-you for Haynes, so he'd best dig them out of his bag while he thought about it.

Chapter 9

The "us" Lieutenant Haynes referred to when he invited Longarm to supper consisted of himself and a slender and very pretty Indian woman who was introduced as Sarah.

Longarm guessed Sarah was somewhat older than her lieutenant's late twenties. Call it somewhere in the neighborhood of thirty or thirty-five. She was, however, not the girl Longarm saw sneaking out of the officers' quarters earlier that day. That girl had very long hair. Sarah's barely reached below her shoulders. Not that it mattered to Longarm if George Haynes cheated on his mistress, nor was it any of Longarm's damned business. He simply smiled in the right places and enjoyed the meal.

And in truth it was a most pleasant repast, especially for such a backwater as this little Army post, with root-crop vegetables, a sort of nut and berry chutney, and a succulent roast of elk to anchor the meal. The cooking and table service was performed by Indians from the Bright Star Reservation and not by soldiers as Longarm would have assumed.

"In case you may be wondering, Deputy, I have a budget allocated for locally procured services. By spending part of it this way I am able to help out a little. Provide jobs for our wards on the reservation, you see."

"They cook for the men as well?" Longarm asked.

"Well, no. The men have too little work to do as it is. Rotating mess duty adds that little bit to the duty roster."

"Yes, of course." Rank does, after all, have its privileges, Longarm silently acknowledged. And if he did not necessarily agree with that ancient dictum of military life . . . no matter. The Army was damn well going to do what they wished and that was just the way it was.

"Do you wish more, uh, uh. . . ." Sarah stopped and groped in her memory for the word she wanted.

"Turnips, dear," Haynes said. "The English for it is turnip."

Sarah smiled. "Yes, turnip. Forgive me, please. My English. Not good. Forgive me."

"Your English is excellent," Longarm said, prompting the woman to beam.

"Thank you. You would like more turnip now? Some *wapiti* maybe so?"

"No, thanks." Longarm leaned back and patted his belly. "I'm full." Turnips were not his most favorite of foods, even when they were flavored with wild onion as these were, and he really was too stuffed to enjoy any more of the elk, which Sarah referred to as *wapiti*.

Sarah said something to the rather dumpy young women who were serving the meal, and they began clearing the table.

Longarm offered Haynes a panatela and Sarah took her cue, excusing herself from the table and withdrawing into the kitchen with the other locals.

"Very pleasant," Longarm said. "Thanks."

48

"It is my pleasure, believe me. We so very seldom get any company here. You don't play cribbage by any chance, do you, Deputy?"

"No. Sorry."

"That's a pity. I haven't found a decent opponent here. I'm afraid I will completely forget how to play if this goes on much longer." He shrugged, then smiled. "But there are compensations."

"Yes, so I gather."

"Will you stay a few days before you start back? I have a few smoothbores we could load with shot. I don't have any bird dog to hunt with, but we could see if we could knock down some prairie chickens for the pot."

"That sounds mighty nice, but I got a job t' do, don't forget. I'll be riding out in the morning."

"Going back so soon? I am truly sorry to hear that, Deputy."

"Oh, I can't go back quite yet, George. I want t' see this reverend of yours in action." He smiled. "Most of all, I'm wantin' to see this amazing transformation you say Many Thumbs has had. That man was one evil son of a bitch when I knew him before. It'd please me no end to see him as a Christian now."

"Do you think it will be necessary to bother with all that? The Reverend Mr. Dascher does not want his spiritual retreat disturbed. He was very clear about that before he took the people away from here. He wants them free to think only about the Word. He wants them to hear only his voice, a voice crying in the wilderness."

Longarm did not know all that much about the subject—and he sure as hell was not going to argue about it with George Haynes—but the way he understood it, it was not Reverend J. Samuel Dascher's voice that was supposed to be crying in the wilderness.

Not that that mattered anyway. Billy Vail told him to go see. There was no way he was going to go back and tell Billy that he had come within a few miles of finding Many Thumbs but stopped short of seeing.

"Thanks for the advice about that, George, but I'll just take a quick look. Won't even have to disturb anybody there. If that's all right with you."

"Oh, it doesn't matter to me, Deputy. Not at all. I was just passing on the request the Reverend Dascher made when he left. No, sir. Doesn't matter a fig to me."

Haynes wadded his napkin and tossed it onto the table, then stood. "If you would excuse me now, sir, I have duties to attend to."

Longarm rose and shook the man's hand. "Thank you for a fine meal, George. I enjoyed it."

"Yes. Of course." Haynes seemed distracted, not really paying much attention to what Longarm was saying.

Longarm left the officer there in the mess hall and ambled outside into the cool of the evening, a canopy of stars bright in the vast sweep of sky overhead.

He thought about having another fine panatela before he turned in, but decided to settle for one of his common cheroots instead. One extra special treat per night ought to be enough to satisfy any man.

Chapter 10

On second thought, Longarm reconsidered a few moments later, two special treats per night should not be considered excessive.

The thing was, there seemed to be a special—quite special indeed—treat waiting for him in the visiting officer's quarters. When he walked in, his bed was already being occupied. And the visitor was really a treat.

The girl sat on the edge of the bunk, naked, her brown skin taking on the golden hue of wild honey in the lamplight. She was slim, with small breasts and an impossibly tiny waist. Black hair fell gleaming to the top of the crack of her round little ass. Her eyes were huge, round, shining.

Her face was not beautiful, but it was lively, animated. Most of all it was . . . friendly. That was it, he decided. This girl looked just plain friendly and likable. Sweet, he supposed, would be another way to put it. She was a girl a man could like.

"Hello."

Her smile was positively radiant. She said something

to him in a tongue he not only did not know, he did not think he had ever heard spoken before now.

"Do you have any English?"

Again she responded in her own language.

Longarm shrugged. He touched his chest and spoke his name.

"Mai," the girl said shyly.

"What are you. . . ." He paused and aloud mumbled, "What am I doing asking you anything? You don't speak a word that I can understand. An' I don't have a word o' whatever it is that you speak."

He stepped across the little room and stopped before her, intending to take her by the hand and point her toward the door. If he could spot her clothes or a blanket or something.

Before he could do that, however, Mai quite matter-of-factly reached for Longarm's fly and began unfastening the buttons there.

"No, look, I don't think this is such a good idea. Y'-know?"

If she knew, she certainly did not act like it. By the time Longarm got the words out, Mai had his cock out of his britches, and the rebellious sonuvabitch of a blind snake was responding without waiting for Custis Long to tell it what he wanted. He got an instant hard-on, hot and throbbing.

Mai saw what he had to work with, and her smile became all the wider. She laughed softly, the sound a furry little chuckle that came from deep in her throat. She leaned forward.

Sitting on the edge of the bunk like she was put her at just the right height. She held his cock and pressed the bulb against her cheek, then rotated her head up and down and from side to side so that his pecker rubbed over her face. She seemed to enjoy the feel of it.

And Longarm damn sure enjoyed what he was feeling. The soft touch of her eyelashes alone near got him off, and when she ever so gently and ever so warmly breathed on him, it sensitized the surface of his pole enough to make him quiver.

When Mai applied the tip of her tongue to the tip of his cock, he jumped. And near squirted all over her face. An involuntary groan escaped from his lips.

Mai said something in a whisper, then leaned forward just a little closer.

Her lips parted to admit the head of his cock, enveloping him with warmth and moisture.

Ever so lightly she rubbed her teeth over his shaft. In and out. Then she held him with her soft lips and mobile tongue only, capturing him with her lips, swirling her tongue around and around.

Longarm felt his hips begin to move in response.

Mai reached up and cupped his balls in the palm of her hand, very gently encouraging his motion and providing the timing that she set for his entry and brief withdrawal.

She pushed forward. Hard and sudden. He felt a tug of resistance as the head of his dick reached the tough ring of cartilage at the entrance to her throat, but Mai continued to press herself onto him until he broke through and was into her throat.

He could feel her nose tight against his belly, and the entire length of his shaft was inside Mai's mouth and throat.

She held him by the balls, wanting him to stay there so deep inside her, then tugged to ask him to back out again.

The air reaching wet skin felt cold. But the heat of her mouth . . .

"You better . . . you better . . ." His breath was becoming rapid and the impulse in his loins uncontrollable. "You better not. . . ."

Mai giggled. And once again impaled her face on Longarm's shaft.

He threw his head back, groaning, and his knees went momentarily weak as he came, hot fluid pouring out of his body and into hers.

Mai swallowed, the constrictions in her throat milking the liquid from him, and her fingers tightened very slightly on his balls.

Longarm cried out. Staggered for a second and grabbed the back of Mai's head to steady himself.

The girl was smiling when she finished draining him and finally withdrew.

Longarm was smiling too if the truth be known.

"That wasn't exactly what I planned, little darlin'," he said.

Mai said something and took his hand, pulling him down to a seat on the bed beside her. Once he was sitting, she snuggled in close against his side with another smile and a contented sigh. She reached down and touched his wet but still upright cock and asked something, then pointed to her own patch of soft, black, curly pubic hair.

Longarm grinned. "Damn right." He nodded. "Just as soon as you give me a moment t' get outa these clothes. An' for Pete's sake, let me get shut of the gunbelt, will you? There are some things a gentleman don't do while he's wearin' a gun." The grin became wider. "Well . . . depends on the kind o' gun you're talkin' about, I suppose."

Mai giggled. And reached down to take a gentle but very firm hold on him. She lay back on his bunk and gleefully spread her knees wide apart, inviting Custis Long to conduct a little exploration in that vicinity.

Longarm made short work of getting out of his duds and accepting the invitation.

Chapter 11

Longarm yawned and slowly stretched. He did not want to wake Mai. After all, the girl had had a rough night. Sort of. Mighty pleasant, though, at least as far as Longarm was concerned. And she acted like she'd enjoyed it more than a little also.

He was giving thought to reaching for that first delicious smoke of the day when he felt the press of a gentle touch.

Mai was awake, and the girl seemed to've awakened in a randy state of mind. Her nipples were erect and her hands were insistent, urging him to rise to the occasion.

Longarm smiled and kissed her. Mai's mouth opened to the probing of his tongue and she arched her back, pressing the softness of her belly against him.

The girl's thighs parted and she tugged Longarm on top of her. His tall, hard frame dwarfed her small body, and he was careful to take most of his weight on his own knees and elbows.

Not that Mai seemed concerned. Her smile became broad when the tip of Longarm's eager cock found its way through the girl's soft fur to the wet opening of her pussy.

He slid forward, giving her time to accommodate his length. She accepted all of it and wrapped her arms and her legs tight around him, her hips pumping in time with Longarm's slow thrusting.

Slow to begin with. Then faster. Faster as passion rose. Faster still as the heat of their joined bodies became overwhelming and Longarm began to build toward a climax.

Faster until all control was abandoned in a brief frenzy of movement, bellies slapping loudly together.

Longarm felt the girl stiffen beneath him. She clutched him with animal strength, her nails digging hard into his back, and she cried out something in her own language. Her head snapped back against the bed and her eyes rolled white as she shuddered and twitched in uncontrolled ecstasy.

Longarm's climax was only moments behind hers. He felt the flow of his sap rise, it seemed, from all the way down to his toes to burst out in a flood.

He spilled his seed into this girl and held himself poised above her for a moment, then with a groan let himself slump down onto her slim body. She cushioned him there, his weight fully on her, his face buried in the cool spill of her hair.

Mai seemed to be unconscious, and Longarm was exhausted, his strength expended inside this girl.

After a few moments—it could not have been long, he thought—he felt Mai stir and begin to move beneath him. Longarm took a deep breath and shook himself, his strength returning as quickly as it fled.

He felt good now. Refreshed. This was not, he thought, a bad way to start a new day.

Mai seemed pleased enough as well. She fairly purred

when she hugged him and said something soft into his ear, wrapping her arms around his neck and holding him there.

"You're a sweet girl an' I like your company just fine, little darlin', but I have work t' do. Now let me up so's I can get dressed and start the day." He smiled and gave her a kiss. The girl reluctantly let go of him, and Longarm stood.

He dressed quickly and strapped on his gunbelt. He closed his saddlebags, but left them where they were for the time being. He intended to see what he could find in the way of a breakfast—he damn sure needed to put some wood in the boiler to make up for what Mai had drained out of him—before he went off to find Many Thumbs and his band of believers.

There was no sign of George Haynes at the mess hall, but the woman called Sarah was there along with several of the Indian kitchen help. That accounted for the telltale smoke Longarm had already noticed hanging over the building.

"Sir, good morning to you," Sarah greeted him, her words accompanied by a smile and a bow.

"Good morning, Sarah."

"You sleep well, I hope."

"Yes, thank you." And if he hadn't gotten all that much actual sleep, well, that hardly seemed to matter.

"You will eat now?"

"Yes, thank you."

Sarah turned and said something and the helpers scurried away. "They will not be long," she said.

"No need t' rush," Longarm told her.

Sarah brightened. "You will stay then? Good. I must tell this to George."

"No, that isn't what I meant." He laughed. "I learned a

long time ago not to make a cook hurry too much. That ain't a good idea at all."

"Oh." Her expression sobered again. "He would have been so pleased if you stay. You will not change your mind? We would make you comfort . . . excuse me, comfortable . . . make you comfortable here. No need for you to go at all."

"Thank you, and I know I'd be comfortable here, but I have my work t' do. I'm sure George understands that."

"Yes, of course. Your food will be ready soon. You excuse me now, please?"

Longarm nodded, and the woman hurried away. Going to wake the lieutenant perhaps. Or whatever. Not that it mattered.

Breakfast proved to be leftover elk roast with rice and gravy and plenty of hot coffee to wash it all down.

Longarm took his time about eating, then headed back to his borrowed quarters. He intended to pick up his gear, then find Haynes to get directions to exactly where the Reverend Mr. Dascher and his flock were supposed to be.

He did not do either of those things. Could not, at least not right away.

When he ducked his head and stepped inside the lean-to, he found the girl Mai sprawled still naked on the bunk, her head tilted over at an impossible angle.

She lay in a pool of congealing blood that was soaking into the mattress and running down onto the floor.

The girl's throat had been slashed so deep, the cut had very nearly taken her head off.

60

Chapter 12

"No, don't touch her. Please. Give me a minute."

The lean-to was the center of attention, not only from the tiny Army garrison, but the reservation Indians as well. That was only to be expected, but the two sides both wanted to claim jurisdiction over the problem, The boss Indian was called John Apple. He was squat and swarthy and looked like he was the sort who himself had slit an awful lot of throats in the past. He wanted to take the girl's body so her people could mourn and give her a proper burial.

George Haynes took one glimpse and promptly threw up. Longarm believed him when he said he'd never seen anything like that before in his life. It seemed an odd admission by an Army officer serving in Indian country during a time when there had been many depredations and violent encounters between the U.S. military and the many Indian tribes, but Haynes did not appear to find anything unusual about it.

The lieutenant kept mumbling about the Army's responsibilities to their "little red brothers" and that the

Army should determine who and what killed the girl known as Mai.

Longarm took him by the sleeve and dragged him inside where the assembled crowd could not overhear.

"Did I hear you say you want to investigate so's you'll know *what* killed this girl, George? D'you mean to tell me you can't figure that out without orders from Washington and an inspector general's report? Well, take a look at the kid's throat an' maybe you can get a clue."

"I mean . . . I just meant . . ."

"Be quiet, George. This situation isn't covered in your manuals. I know. I've read those same manuals. One of the things they'll tell you is that the Army don't investigate crimes on Indian reservations. But U.S. marshals do. Which happens t' be me. So I want you t' go back outside and huddle up with John Apple. I want you t' tell that man over an' over an' over again how very sorry the United States Army and the War Department and the President of the United States all are about the death of this girl, an' I want you to tell him that quick as I get done in here you are gonna release the girl's body to her people so's they can bury her.

"Can you do that, George? Can you apologize all t' hell and gone, please? And while you're out there, send your soldier boys on their way. Send 'em someplace else. Anyplace else. We don't want them here carrying rifles and making the Indians even more nervous than they already are. Would you do that, please?"

"I, um, if you think best. I suppose."

"Attaboy, George. Now go out there an' take charge of your soldiers and have your talk with John Apple and leave me alone for just a little while. I'll let Apple know when he can have the body."

"All right. Yes, I will do that."

62

"Thank you, George. Go on now." Longarm half-pushed the officer out, then turned his attention back to the dead girl.

There was little enough to see that he hadn't already known in that first glance. Mai quite obviously was killed while Longarm was having breakfast, and it was just as obvious what brutal, bloody, completely effective method the killer chose.

The girl either had had no time to start getting dressed after Longarm left, or perhaps she had decided to stay as she was while she got a little sleep. Perhaps she even hoped for another round of lovemaking when Longarm came back to collect his gear from the visiting officer's quarters.

Longarm examined her hands. There were no cuts there to indicate she tried to ward off the knife that killed her and no scraped skin under her fingernails, at least none that he could find.

He pressed his fingers against the ball of her chin, the flesh feeling loose and spongy to the touch now that there could be no muscle reaction, and pushed her head to the side.

Drying blood obscured the wound, so he fetched the hand towel from the washstand nearby and tipped a little water into the basin there, then dampened one end of the towel. He went back to Mai and used the wet cloth to wipe the blood away from the deep, ugly wound.

The cut was clean, he saw. More interesting, it was continuous in one motion, with neither false starts nor repeated cuts. There had been no sawing, just the one very quick swipe of the blade.

Mai had not resisted her killer, so she either knew her attacker and expected no harm or was asleep at the time. Either way, this had been an unpleasant way to die. Blood covered her hands, wrists, and forearms, which told him she'd reached up to the wound and tried without success to stanch the gushing flood of arterial blood.

She was as good as dead as soon as her assailant struck, though. Nothing could have been done for her after that, not even if a team of the Army's best surgeons had been standing by ready to help.

One quick, hard slash and Mai was dead.

But why?

That was a question mere physical evidence was unlikely to answer. Even if there was evidence left behind, and in this instance Longarm saw nothing, no footprints or conveniently dropped objects to tell him who it was who committed this murder.

He did look, though. He looked carefully around the room, under the bed, behind each piece of furniture. He moved Mai's body to one side of the narrow bunk and back to the other hoping—but in truth not expecting—to find something that would give him a direction to start in.

There was nothing.

When Longarm was completely satisfied that he had learned all he could, he went outside. Haynes was still out there, still apologizing to John Apple as Longarm had directed. At this point he sounded more like he was groveling than merely apologizing, though. Longarm joined the two, the Army lieutenant and the Indian chief, and put a merciful end to Haynes's embarrassment. By God, though, Longarm thought, if the Army ever needed men to specialize in surrender, George here would be just their man. Hell, he probably should resign from the Army and join up with the diplomatic corps. Groveling was their main strength. Or seemed to be.

"You can take her now," Longarm told John Apple.

"With our apologies," Haynes added.

Apple nodded and spoke to the throng of Indians who were standing around looking more and more threatening. Not a few of them were showing weapons at this point, hatchets and war clubs and short buffalo lances. It would be one hell of a mess if they decided to forget peace and turn loose, Longarm realized. George Haynes's boys in blue would last maybe four minutes before their scalps were dangling in the breeze, and after that there would not be another deterrent force for fifty or a hundred miles in any direction.

It was a disquieting thought.

"Ask your people who might have done this, John Apple. Someone may know."

"Huh. So'jers. You ask so'jers who do this thing," John Apple countered.

"I will ask them, John Apple, and if I do not know after that, I will ask your people too. But first it will be good for you to ask because they trust you. I am only a stranger and a white man. It is better if you ask. And I will talk with the soldiers while you are doing that."

John Apple grunted. He looked skeptical about this whole thing, but he nodded. "This I will do. You have my word."

"And your word is good, John Apple. Thank you."

A few moments later, after Mai's body was carried away with the Indians trudging along with her, Haynes turned to Longarm and said, "Indians lie, you know. John Apple is no different when it comes to that."

"White men lie too, George. That doesn't mean questions aren't worth asking. Now if you please, I'd like your men, all of them, to report to the mess hall. I'll want to talk with them. In private, one at a time."

"All right, but as their commanding officer I expect to be present at any interrogation you conduct."

"You'll stand outside with everybody else, Lieutenant," Longarm ordered in a crisp, no-nonsense tone of voice. "I will speak with the men one at a time and in private. And before you ask, no, I will not report these conversations to you afterward. Whatever they may say to me will be privately held between them an' me."

Haynes pulled his shoulders back. "Yes, sir."

Chapter 13

Longarm assembled the men by squad and brought them into the mess hall one at a time in the same order they were lined up in, the privates first and their corporals after them. He spoke with Corporal Tom Brawley's squad first, a rather nervous George Haynes pacing back and forth outside, then released the squad to the lieutenant for duty.

"You can send your people in now, Corporal," he told Ed Lassiter. "One at a time, if you please."

"Yes, sir."

Longarm returned to his seat at the far end of a mess table that was able to accommodate forty men or so. He wanted to be far enough away from the door to give the men confidence that there would be no eavesdropping. Even so, he found no one who admitted to any knowledge of the killer. No one saw anything out of the ordinary. No one heard any noises coming from the visiting officer's quarters that morning.

Longarm treated each man as if he were the first and only potential witness, resisting the temptation to hurry through an interview on the assumption that he would surely learn nothing anyway simply because none of the others had anything of value to offer.

The soldiers were mostly cooperative if somewhat indifferent to the death of the Indian girl. All of them acknowledged remembering the pleasant young girl. But then she'd had the sort of personality that would make her stand out in any group, red or white. None of the soldiers admitted to having sex with her. None of them knew of anyone else, white or red, having relations with Mai.

Longarm began to wonder just why in hell Mai had chosen to slip into his bed last night when she seemed never to have done such a thing for anyone before that time.

More to the point, who would it have been who sent her to him? And why?

"Thank you, Hassan," he told a young private from Indiana. "You can go now. And ask the next man to come in, please."

The soldier stood and picked up his cap. "There isn't nobody else, sir. I'm the last one in the squad. Well, 'cept for the corp'rul, that is."

"Then ask the corporal to come in."

"Yes, sir."

Hassan left and a few moments later Ed Lassiter came inside.

"Shut the door please, Ed, and take a seat." Longarm pulled out a pair of cheroots and offered one to Lassiter. There was something about the corporal that made Longarm think he was reliable and probably honest as well. Maybe it was just that he found the man to be likable in much the same easygoing manner that Mai had been likable. "I think there's some leftover coffee on the stove in there," he said, nodding in the direction of the kitchen end of the long mess hall. "Have some if you like."

"No, thank you, sir. I'm fine."

"You seem tense today, Ed. Kinda stiff. Is everything all right? Other than the fact that a girl was killed this morning, that is." Longarm scratched a match aflame and held it to light Lassiter's cheroot, then applied the flame to his own. He took his time about drawing in a long, pleasant draught of smoke, then leaned back in his chair.

"I've asked the same things to all the other men, Ed. They all say they remember that girl, but the way they tell it she might as well've been a virgin. No one ever saw her with a man, not even an Indian suitor. Why are they telling me a thing like that, Ed? Has someone"— Longarm was careful to avoid suggesting who "someone" might be—"has someone suggested it would be a good thing if nobody knows anything about this?"

"No, *sir*!" Lassiter barked in a tone of voice that was clearly parade-ground rote.

Longarm smiled and winked through a wreath of pale smoke. "Not. . . . um . . . exactly. Is that it?"

The corporal glanced around to make sure the door was closed and they were alone. "That isn't what I said, sir. Not. . . . um . . . exactly."

"The girl's name was Mai, wasn't it?"

"So I understood, yes, sir."

"And she was the girl I saw slipping out of the lieutenant's quarters yesterday afternoon, wasn't she?"

"Oh, I couldn't comment on anything you might've seen, sir, because I wouldn't of been the one as did the seeing."

"But Mai was with the lieutenant yesterday, wasn't she?"

"She might have been. I couldn't swear to it, sir."

"I'm not asking you to swear to anything, Ed. I'm just setting here having a talk, just you an' me, nobody else around. And whatever you say won't be leaving this room." Longarm sat smoking in silence for a few moments, then said, "Loyalty is a good thing, Ed. I respect it. But sometimes there's a question about who you're gonna be loyal to, the uniform or the man. The uniform an' the country it serves or the individual who wears that uniform. If you know what I mean."

"Yes, sir. I guess I do."

"Yesterday I got the impression that you are a good soldier."

"I try to be, sir."

"Mai was that girl, wasn't she?"

"It . . . could be, sir. I couldn't say for certain sure."

"All right. Fair enough. But it's pretty plain that Mai was entertaining the lieutenant yesterday afternoon even though no one wants to admit that. The thing that puzzles me, though, isn't so much the girl Mai but the woman called Sarah. Does she mind the lieutenant having girls on the side like that?"

Lassiter laughed, a puff of smoke bursting out of his mouth and obscuring his face for a moment. He began to cough. Longarm waited until the coughing subsided.

"Sir, Sarah ain't the lieutenant's woman. She's the boss of them Indians. The whole lot of 'em."

"Sarah? What about John Apple? I thought he was the chief."

"Oh, he is. He's the . . . I dunno. I guess you could say John Apple is kinda like the mayor of a town. But he ain't the real boss. The real boss is that Sarah. She's the one really runs things around here."

"Even the lieutenant?"

70

"I didn't say that, sir."

"Not exactly, you didn't."

"No, sir. Not exactly."

"If John Apple is the mayor, then what is Sarah?"

"Oh, it's easy enough to say what Sarah is, sir. She's a witch! An' I don't mean you should take that like I'm trying to avoid saying she's a bitch. Because she ain't no way no bitch nor anything like it. What I mean is that the woman is a witch. A really and truly witch."

"I'll be damn," Longarm mumbled as he drew on his cheroot.

Chapter 14

Lieutenant George Haynes was waiting outside the mess hall when Longarm finished talking with the enlisted men. The process had taken hours, but Haynes was still there although the men had been sent off to their duties. "Well, were your interviews helpful?" Haynes asked as he fell into step beside Longarm on their way back to the headquarters building. "Did you learn anything?"

"No," Longarm told him, "not a damn thing unfortunately. They all remember having seen the girl from time to time around the reservation, but no one remembers anything special about her. And no one seems to 've seen or heard anything out of the ordinary this morning."

"She was found in quarters that were assigned for your use," Haynes said, stating the obvious.

"That's where she spent the night," Longarm told him.

The lieutenant's stride faltered and his jaw dropped open. He seemed genuinely shocked, Longarm thought. No one could be that good an actor. Haynes really had not known that his afternoon playmate was in there fucking Longarm.

Haynes recovered quickly enough and regained control of himself, his expression betraying nothing of what he felt about the girl's betrayal of him. He cleared his throat and said, "Not that it is any of my business, of course. I did not mean to intrude."

"No offense taken, Lieutenant. I only mentioned it because it's the reason she was there this morning. I left her alone there when I dressed and went to breakfast."

"Do you think the murderer expected to find you there and killed the girl . . . what was her name? Do you happen to know? Expected to find you, do you think, and killed the girl so she could not identify him as an intruder?"

"That's always possible," Longarm said, although he did not for a minute believe it. "Her name was Mai, by the way."

"Ah, yes. Thank you. I shall have to remember that for my report of the incident."

And Custis Long was going to believe that George Haynes spent his afternoons romping between Mai's legs but never knew her name. Sure he did. If that little scrap of information ever made it into an official report, it wouldn't likely be one written for the War Department, it would be one submitted to U.S. Marshal William Vail.

"Now what?" Haynes asked as he stepped inside headquarters, reaching up by habit to remove his hat—never wear it indoors unless reporting for duty—and hang it on a coat tree. Haynes sank onto his chair and straightened his back. He seemed more comfortable and to feel more in charge once he was behind his desk.

"I'll go over this afternoon an' talk to John Apple. Maybe interview some o' the Indians if I can find some that speak English." Longarm smiled. "Find some that admit to it, that is."

"Yes, well, if I can do anything to help, I and the men of this command are at your disposal, sir."

"I appreciate that, Lieutenant. Now if you'll excuse me, I need t' go find where your boys put my horse." It was only a few hundred yards to the near edge of the reservation encampment, but the clusters of buffalo-hide lodges were scattered over an area a mile or more long.

"Anything to help," Haynes repeated rather weakly, his attention wandering and turning inward.

Longarm could not help but wonder if the officer had developed serious affections for his little dusky mistress. Falling in love with an Indian girl would be sure death for his career. But then it did not appear that George Haynes had much of a career to lose. And he did seem to be taking Mai's death hard, although it was impossible to tell whether it was her murder or the fact that she spent her last night on earth cuckolding him that bothered the man.

Longarm returned to the visiting officer's quarters to find very little evidence remained of Mai's rather messy death. While he was busy talking with the enlisted men, someone had scrubbed most of the blood away from the floorboards, although a dark stain would be there as long as the floor was. The mattress had been taken away, leaving nothing but the bed frame and laced support ropes inside it.

His gear appeared to have been undisturbed, but he took a moment to glance through it anyway. He could see no evidence of tampering, and his Winchester—he checked—was still fully loaded.

Not that he expected that anything would be amiss. But it never hurts to apply a little caution.

Longarm took a handful of cheroots from his rapidly diminishing supply and stuffed them into a pocket. He needed some sort of gift to take to John Apple and the cheroots were the best he could manage under the circumstances.

He headed for the stable to collect his horse and saddle, leaving the Winchester and other gear where they were.

Chapter 15

John Apple sat cross-legged on a blanket, smoking one of Longarm's cheroots. The two of them were seated on opposite sides of a small fire contained within a ring of stones. Longarm could not help but notice that the ring for this "council fire" was so freshly dug that the dirt was still damp. This was not the band's accepted fire pit. But then at that site John Apple might feel honor-bound to speak the truth.

Another deviation from custom and hospitality was that they were holding their discussion outdoors, close to a collection of scalp poles. Ordinarily, Longarm would have expected to be invited into John Apple's lodge to smoke and share food before they got down to the serious business of conversation.

This was not exactly an insult. But it wasn't very damn far from it.

"You have spoken with all your people?" Longarm asked.

John Apple nodded solemnly. "I have sent out a call among our peoples. I have talked with our young men and with their fathers, their uncles, their grandfathers. No one of these people knows who murdered the girl Yellow Flowers at Sunrise."

"Yellow Flo . . . I thought her name was Mai."

Apple nodded. "It was her . . . what would you call it? Her small name."

"Nickname?" Longarm suggested.

"Yes. Nickname."

"What about her family? Did you speak with them? Do they know if she had enemies?"

"I speak. This girl was without enemy. She brought sunshine to all who were near."

"Yes," Longarm agreed. "That is how she was. Do you have any thoughts about who could have killed her?"

"Could have? Any soldier *could* have done this thing and a hundred or more of our people *could* have. I do not know who *did* kill."

"Did you talk with Sarah? Does she know?"

"Snow Maiden has closed the flap on her lodge and there is the scent of magic in the smoke that comes from it. Perhaps it is the killer of Yellow Flowers at Sunrise that she seeks in her dreaming."

"If she learns anything I hope you will tell me, John Apple."

The Indian nodded. "It will be so."

Unless, Longarm thought, Sarah—Snow Maiden—instructed him otherwise.

Sitting there looking into John Apple's face, Longarm had no idea if the man was telling him the truth about . . . well, about any of the things he said. It could all be just so much bullshit or it could be gospel. Longarm simply could not judge.

"I am sorry for the loss," Longarm said.

John Apple only shrugged. "It happened. There is no way to change what is."

Longarm grunted. But he could not accept the girl's death so readily, could not be so lacking in emotion. Quite apart from the fact that the murder was a crime and it was his job to investigate it, this particular murder was a personal thing with him. It had to be. The girl spent her last hours bringing him happiness; then she was murdered in his own bed with his juices still warm inside her small body while Longarm, who should have been there to protect her, sat calmly eating his breakfast just a few rods distant.

The fact was that this murder had become a very personal thing with him and he intended to find the killer whether John Apple . . . or Sarah . . . or any-damn-one else wanted him to.

"I will inform the Great Father how you have treated me here, John Apple, so that he can know this thing before commodities are next assigned for your people," Longarm said solemnly, careful to avoid mentioning just what he might say in his official report. He was sure John Apple would notice that oversight. If the man wanted to worry about it, and about how it might affect the future of the Bright Star Reservation, well, so be it.

Longarm stood, the cartilage in his knees cracking after having been sitting there cross-legged for so long a time, and headed back to the Army post.

Chapter 16

"Can I do anything for you, sir?"

"No thanks, Corporal, I . . . wait a minute. I'd like to change my mind about that. In fact there is something."

"Yes, sir?"

"Would you please have one of your men bring my horse around. There is something that I want to do."

"Of course, sir. Wait here." Corporal Brawley came to attention, snapped his heels together, then executed a proper about-face and marched away toward the stables.

The man—all of the men on the post—were walking on eggshells when they were around him now, Longarm noticed. He frowned, wondering why. Were they nervous about the fact that there had been a murder on the post? Or did they perhaps wonder just how much this outsider, this peace officer with the authority to investigate and to arrest, knew . . . or might come to know?

*Some*one here had plenty to hide.

Longarm just wished to hell he knew who that was.

And what they were trying to accomplish when they killed Yellow Flowers at Sunrise.

That girl had not died as the result of some argument or catfight. The killing was coldly premeditated. That much was clear from the evidence that there was no attempt on the victim's part to defend herself or to fight back.

Either she trusted her attacker, or possibly she had dropped off to sleep. Longarm wished he knew which.

With a sigh, he acknowledged that he did not know. And likely never would until or unless he could find the killer and ask him.

A soldier wearing a dirty white canvas uniform appeared, leading Longarm's saddled mount. "The corporal said I should bring him to you, sir."

"Thank you . . . Bradley, isn't it?"

The soldier beamed. The marshal had remembered his name and it pleased him. "Yes, sir, thank you, sir."

There was no way Longarm was going to admit now that he could not recall if Bradley was the man's first name or last. By way of unspoken atonement for his lapse of memory, he pulled two cheroots out of his coat pocket and offered one to Bradley before nipping off the tip of his own, striking a match, and lighting both smokes. At this rate the cheroots were not going to last long. Not that he begrudged handing out a cigar now and then. He just hoped there was something available on the post to replace them if or when he ran out.

"Thank you, sir. Thank you very much."

"My pleasure, Bradley." Longarm accepted the reins from the man, and the private held the horse's headstall while Longarm mounted.

"Should I tell the lieutenant you'll be back in time for supper, sir?"

"I don't know when I'll be back, so I don't see any need for you to tell him anything at all unless he asks."

"Oh, he's already asked, sir. That's why I wanted to know. Sort of, that is."

"He knows I asked for my horse?"

"Yes, sir. The lieutenant gave orders that he's to be kept informed of anything you need." Bradley looked embarrassed and quickly added, "We're to give you anything you want, of course. The lieutenant said that too. We're all to help you any way we can."

"But he wants to know about it," Longarm said.

"Yes, sir. That too. I hope you don't mind, sir."

"I don't mind at all. I am sure he's just trying to be as helpful as possible."

"Yes, sir, that's it exactly. Helpful."

"Right, well, you can tell him that I don't know exactly when I will be back."

"And, uh, can I tell him where it is that you'll be going, sir?"

Longarm smiled. "That would be hard t' do, Bradley, since you don't know." Longarm kneed the horse forward and very quickly put the animal into a lope before the soldier could ask anything more about his plans.

Hell, Longarm didn't have any actual plans. He just wanted to get away from the dreary sights and smells at Bright Star, get off to where he could breathe deep of some clean air and do a little thinking.

But there was no reason why George Haynes or any of his people needed to know that.

Someone on this reservation—someone red or someone white, it didn't matter—someone here had cause to worry about what Deputy Marshal Custis Long might be up to.

Let 'em worry, Longarm figured. Let them fret and

fuss until they talked themselves into making a mistake.

And when they did, dammit, he intended to be there to see that the son of a bitch paid for the murder of one very nice and ever-smiling little Indian girl.

Chapter 17

Longarm spent the next day and a half interviewing people and in general making himself visible. The truth was
that he did not have a clue about who the murderer was or
why the girl had been killed. What he hoped to do was to
spook the killer into making a mistake—a small one
would do—that would expose the son of a bitch.

The ploy failed miserably. The killer either had nerves
of tempered steel . . . or was no longer on the reservation.
Either of those was possible.

"I'll be riding out in the morning," he announced at
dinner that night.

"You are leaving?" George Haynes sounded surprised.
"I thought you intended to find whoever killed Mai."

"I do, but I need t' look at all the Bright Star folks.
Whoever done that girl in coulda slipped over to the Reverend Dascher's camp thinking to get away with the
killing. I'll poke around over there some an' see what I
come up with."

Longarm did indeed intend to pursue his investigation
there, along with completing the assignment Billy Vail

gave him to begin with. In addition to that, however, he was hoping that his departure would give the killer some sense of security. And hoping that that in turn would lead to the mistake that would expose the murderer.

At least that was his hope. Certainly it could accomplish no less than he was getting done here on the reservation.

Haynes said nothing more about it, but he did not appear to be happy with Longarm's plan.

For his part, Longarm prepared for the ride to Dascher's camp by taking a third helping of the roast elk, and afterward Sarah served a wine—something called a Tokay—that wasn't entirely terrible even if Longarm was not generally much for wine. Snow Maiden even relaxed from her duties long enough to take a seat at the table with them and to share a very small taste of the golden Tokay before retiring while the gentlemen had cigars and coffee.

"It's getting late," Longarm said when his social obligations had been met and he could make his escape without being rude. "I'm gonna turn in now. I may feel like getting an early start tomorrow morning, so I'd best say my good-byes now."

The lieutenant's handshake was weak and his expressions of regret perfunctory. That was all right. Longarm did not like George Haynes any more than the officer liked him. The acquaintance was strictly duty-related. As soon as he decently could, Longarm slipped out into the night and made his way back to his room.

The moon was not yet up and there was little light in the sky, but that little was much more than was in the lean-to that served here as visiting officer's quarters. Longarm left the door open so he would not be in complete darkness while he fumbled and stumbled his way to the lamp stand.

He managed to grasp the lamp without knocking it over, lifted the glass chimney, and touched a match to the wick. He replaced the chimney, adjusted the wick, and turned to find that the bed frame was still bare. The blood-soaked mattress had been taken away by whoever it was who cleaned up in here, but no replacement had been brought in. Not that it mattered. Longarm sometimes thought he had spent more nights sleeping without a bed than in one.

He dropped his Stetson on the latticework of ropes laced inside the frame and looked around the room for a good spot to lay out his bedroll. For sure he was not going to place it over those ropes. He had slept on bare beds more than once in the past and did not like it. Without a proper mattress the ropes cut into a person, and after a few hours could hurt like all billy hell. He could do without that, thank you.

He lighted the evening's final cheroot from the lamp flame and crossed the tiny room to push the door closed. The latch was broken, he noticed, probably jostled by one of the soldiers who cleaned up. No matter, he thought. Without the wooden latch the door tended to swing open of its own weight, so he held it closed and used the toe of his boot to drag a spittoon over and push it against the bottom of the door. That would hold it closed unless an awfully strong wind came up.

Longarm unfastened his bedroll and rolled it out on the floor, then dug in his bag for the bottle of rye whiskey he kept there. The Maryland distilled rye tasted one hell of a lot better going down than the after-dinner wine had. It cleaned his mouth and warmed his belly. Did such a good job of both that he had a second swig out of the bottle, then replaced the cork and carefully tucked the bottle away again.

He sat for a few minutes while he finished his smoke, gave thought to the rye but left it where it was, then stripped down to his balbriggans and blew the lamp flame out, plunging the small room into total darkness.

Longarm felt his way to the bedroll and lay down with a yawn and a contented stretch to loosen tight muscles.

Tomorrow he would have to . . . the hell with it. He would worry about tomorrow when it came. In the meantime, he intended to get a good long sleep.

Chapter 18

Damn rats. He could hear one scratching at the floor. *Skritch-skritch-skritch.* Miserable, filthy, nasty little sons of bitches. They . . .

Longarm snapped the rest of the way to wakefulness in a heart-pounding rush.

That was no fucking rat! That was the sound of something very slowly and surreptitiously being dragged across the floorboards.

It took him a moment to identify the faint noise. It was the spittoon he'd used to prop the door closed. Someone was very slowly and cautiously pushing the door open an inch or two at a time.

Longarm sat up, sliding his heavy Colt out of the leather as he did so.

There was some moonlight outside now. Enough for him to see the black shape of the door and a pale bar of moonlight that grew wider with each new scrape of the brass spittoon across hard wood.

Moving silently, he stood and slipped close to the wall.

A head seen in dark silhouette appeared from behind the door. Then an arm and shoulder.

And a hand with a knife in it.

The murderer come a-calling? It looked like it. Damned convenient too.

Longarm reversed the Colt so that his hand was wrapped around the cylinder and the flat of the grip was held as if a club. One good whack and he would have some answers while the tribe had their killer.

He took a half step forward and raised the Colt to strike.

The assassin whirled. Whether the killer heard him, smelled him, or just somehow sensed he was there, Longarm did not know. Whatever the reason, there was a huff of breath like a gasp in the night.

The knife flashed, seeking Longarm's belly to dump his guts onto the floor.

Instinctively he darted backward, sucking his stomach in tight—and puckering his asshole if the truth be known—while he struck down with the clubbed revolver.

Steel met flesh and he heard the dull, ugly sound of snapping bone.

The killer cried out, and the knife clattered harmlessly onto the floor. Longarm lunged forward and wrapped his arms around the kicking, squirming, sobbing assassin.

The killer was . . . the killer was a girl. A small one at that, with waist-length hair and tiny little nubbins for tits. As Longarm discovered from hanging onto her. He doubted she would go more than eighty pounds on the scale, but she was a scrappy little spitfire. It was all he could do to hold onto her, and at that she gave his shins fits, stomping with her heels and twisting around trying to bite him. It was damned lucky she was wearing moccasins, or he would have had scrapes and bruises enough to match a train wreck.

"Whoa, dammit. Hold still. I ain't gonna hurt you."

The girl tried to bite him again and said something that it was just as well he did not understand. From the tone of her voice, he doubted that he wanted to know the meaning of those particular words.

"Will you for cryin' out loud hold *still*!"

She twisted around to face him and tried to plant a knee in his nuts. If she insisted on playing rough. . . .

Longarm grabbed a handful of the hair that was flying in his face and yanked. The girl cried out in pain and went to her knees.

Quick before she could set herself, Longarm grabbed for her arm to turn her around so she could not kick him. The reaction he got was not what he expected. The girl screamed in obvious agony, shuddered, and passed out cold.

It was only then that he remembered her broken arm. The arm that he was holding now.

Feeling half ashamed of himself, never mind that the girl came in here with the apparent intent to kill him, he picked her up and placed her onto thc bare rope "springs" on the cot in the lean-to.

He found a match and snapped it aflame. In its faint glow he could see that the girl was little more than a child. In her teens, he guessed, with a flat face and pimples.

Whatever in the hell was she . . .

The burning match reached his fingertips and he snarled as he quickly dropped it, then lighted another. This time he applied the flame to the wick of the lamp beside the bed and adjusted it to a softly purring butterfly.

In the lamplight he could get a better look at the girl.

He was fairly sure he had never seen her before, although it was remotely possible that she might have been one of the kitchen help and he'd just never noticed her. She was not, in truth, the sort of girl he would notice. She was as plain as a church mouse. And not very accomplished as an assassin.

Longarm sighed. Perhaps he should revise that opinion. It was entirely possible, even quite likely, that this girl was the one who murdered Yellow Flowers at Sunrise. They were not all that far apart in age, he supposed. There could be a thousand reasons why one young girl would want to lash out at another, starting with simple jealousy. After all, Mai had been vivaciously attractive, while this girl would hardly be noticeable in a room full of potato sacks.

Whatever her reasons, he would know them soon enough, he figured. As soon as she woke up, he would find someone who spoke her language so they could get some answers. And some peace.

The whole reservation, he figured, would be pleased to put this mess behind them.

And Custis Long could get about the job that brought him here.

He turned to poke his head out the door. He ought to be able to scare up the corporal of the guard—surely Lieutenant Haynes had not relaxed military discipline to the extent that he was no longer bothering to post guards overnight—to take charge of this girl while Longarm rounded up some Indians to help, John Apple perhaps, or Snow Maiden.

It was Corporal Tom Brawley who came out rubbing sleepy eyes and hastily pulling his suspender straps over his shoulders. His shirttail dangled outside the waistband of his trousers and he was in need of a shave.

"Yes, sir."

"Get Lieutenant Haynes for me, Brawley."

"The lieutenant, he don't like to be waked up before reveille, sir. Not 'less it's a real emergency."

"Thank you for that information, Corporal. Now get the lieutenant for me." Longarm's voice hardened. "Do it *now!*"

"Yes, sir." Brawley stumbled off into the darkness.

Longarm went back indoors and grabbed his clothes to ward off the nighttime chill in the air outside. He also remembered to search on the floor until he finally located the knife the girl had been carrying. It had skittered underneath the washstand and it took him a while to find it. He tucked it behind his gunbelt. Not that he likely had to worry about it. The girl was still out cold, and did not look like she had moved a hair since he'd placed her on the cot.

Once he was dressed, he went back outside. The corporal of the guard was on his way back from the commanding officer's quarters. Brawley looked wide awake now.

"Lieutenant Haynes's compliments, sir. He will meet you in the mess hall in ten minutes."

"The mess hall?"

Brawley shrugged. "It's the lieutenant's way, sir. He's hard to get wokened up. Can't hardly find his ass with both hands till he's had his first quart of coffee."

"All right. There's nothing you can do to change his routine, but I expect maybe I can. In the meantime, Corporal, I want you to stand in this doorway. No one comes in and for damn sure that girl don't go out."

Brawley leaned past Longarm's shoulder and peered into the lighted room behind him where the girl was passed out on the bare bed.

"You want I should, um, do anything with her, sir?"

93

Longarm had too good an idea of the kinds of things the corporal might choose to do to an unconscious young female. "No, Brawley, I want you to stand in the doorway. Like I said, no one in an' no one out. That is the extent of your assignment."

"Yes, sir."

Longarm fetched his Winchester—it was entirely possible that the girl might awaken, and he did not want to leave any weapons for her—and headed for the mess hall.

The truth was that he could stand a cup of coffee himself, and with Brawley standing guard at the door, the girl was not going anywhere.

Longarm reached into his coat pocket for a cheroot and a match. He was wide awake now. But then someone trying to murder you can have that effect on a man, or so he had noticed in the past.

Chapter 19

Haynes was halfway through his first cup by the time Longarm arrived. "Sit down, Marshal," the officer invited, standing politely and pointing to a chair. "Would you like coffee?"

"Sure. That sounds good, thanks." Longarm laid the Winchester on the table and sat.

Haynes walked into the kitchen end of the mess hall, and returned with a huge enamelware pot and another cup. He poured for Longarm, then topped off his own cup before he resumed his seat.

Longarm laced his with sugar and tinned milk, then took an exploratory sip. He scowled. "What the hell? This shit is cold as a gold-camp whore's heart."

Lieutenant Haynes chuckled. "You didn't think we would waste wood to keep the stove hot all night, did you? My standing order is for a fresh pot to be made the last thing in the evening and set atop the stove. When it cools off, well, so it does. But at least I have my coffee first thing. I don't have to wait until the stove heats up and the water boils."

"But damn, man, it gets bitter as gall when you do that," Longarm protested.

"Yes it does, doesn't it?" Haynes said with a nod and a laugh.

"You don't mind that?"

"Bad coffee is better than none," the lieutenant said. "Don't you agree?"

Longarm sighed. And agreed.

"Now tell me," Haynes said. "Why is it that you had me roused out of a warm bed to come here and drink this terrible coffee, eh?"

Longarm was filling him in on the problem when Sarah slipped quietly into the mess hall. She came and stood beside Haynes's shoulder while Longarm finished explaining about the attempt on his life.

"Do you know who she is?" Haynes asked when Longarm was done.

Before Longarm had a chance to answer, Sarah—Snow Maiden—spoke. "She is Three Shells. She is of the Bannock tribe."

"Why would she want to murder the marshal here?" Haynes asked. "Does she even know him?"

"I do not know why she would harm our guest. I can speak with her if you wish."

"Yes, please."

"When you are done with your coffee," Sarah said. She drifted away, moving with the grace and the silence of a ghost, and began rebuilding the fire in the kitchen stove.

Haynes shrugged and picked up his cup. "I'll just drink this down and we can go over there," he said.

Longarm tried a tentative sip of his again. And again made a face. It was wretched stuff. Vile. On the other hand, it was also the only coffee available until a fresh pot was boiled. He took another swallow, deeper this time. Maybe he would get used to it, he told himself.

Twenty minutes later, George Haynes was finished with his morning ritual of the coffeepot and Sarah was done fiddling about in the kitchen. "We can go now," the Indian woman announced, as if she were the one in charge here and not the officer.

Haynes obediently stood and followed her to the door, Longarm tagging along behind them.

A pale glow to the east suggested that dawn would not be long in coming.

Corporal Brawley came to attention and saluted when his commanding officer approached. "Begging the lieutenant's pardon, sir, but I haven't woken the troops yet. The marshal here said I was to stand guard right here so that's what I done."

"That's fine, Corporal, you did the right thing."

"Can I go shake them out now?"

"Yes, but don't be too long about it. I will want you and a detail of two men to escort the prisoner back to her own people as soon as we've had a chance to interview her."

"Yes, sir. Right away, sir." The corporal headed toward the barracks at double time. Longarm noticed that the members of the Indian kitchen staff were arriving for their day's work now, and there was a curl of dense smoke coming from the stovepipe on the mess hall roof. He hoped they would break out some bacon for breakfast. And some flapjacks. That would be . . .

"Marshal!" There was a note of alarm in Haynes's voice.

Longarm saw the reason for that the moment he joined the lieutenant at the lean-to doorway.

The girl was still there. But there would be no interrogation. Not today or any day. Once again the rope-sprung cot held a young woman's body. And once again the body was awash in blood. Or, more accurately, the room was. This time there was no mattress to soak up the blood. This time it spread like a crimson carpet across half or more of the floor area, so fresh that it had not yet begun to coagulate and clot as it dried.

"Aw, shit!" Longarm groaned.

Chapter 20

"No, don't go in there, please," Longarm said, taking Haynes by the elbow when the officer started forward into the lean-to.

"Why?"

"Because I wanta figure out who done this, that's why. I don't need you making footprints all through that blood. Let's do this nice an' slow an' thorough." He shook his head. "God knows there ain't no need to hurry. Not now there ain't. Where was it Brawley went to?"

"The barracks. He will be back in a little while with that detail that is supposed to escort the girl back to her camp."

"Sarah, would you mind asking the corporal to come here," Longarm said.

The Indian woman seemed quite startled that Longarm would be asking her to perform a chore for him. She drew back, her expression hard and her chin and shoulders braced. Then she appeared to reconsider. Her posture and her expression returned to her relaxed, if slightly haughty, normal demeanor. "Yes, of course." She turned and moved away with that peculiarly fluid, almost floating gait she sometimes employed.

"Brawley was standing guard at the door the whole time, wasn't he?" Haynes said.

"He was s'posed to be. The last time I looked in, the girl was just fine an' Brawley was wide awake. I wouldn't think he'd 've dropped off to sleep while the two of us was having coffee. Even if he did, you'd think he woulda surely heard something if somebody slipped in there an' killed her."

"Surely you don't think Brawley killed her," Haynes said. "The corporal is one of my best people. I trust him completely. And he would have no reason to kill the girl."

"None that you an' me know about," Longarm agreed. He fished around inside his coat, found a cheroot there. It was bent and slightly battered from being carried too long, but there was only one break in the wrapper. He could still smoke it as long as he held his finger over that spot. Longarm was a good inch and a half into his wounded cigar when Sarah reappeared, Thomas Brawley trailing close at her heels.

The Indian woman joined them. Brawley came to attention and saluted his commanding officer. "The, um, the lady said you wanted to see me, sir? Right away?"

Haynes nodded and returned the salute. "At ease, Tom. The marshal here has some questions for you."

Brawley relaxed and turned to face Longarm. "Yes, sir?" When he did so, he got a look inside the lean-to. "Good God! What happened?"

"You can see what happened to the prisoner you were guarding, Corporal."

"I . . . I don't understand, sir. What happened here? When did it happen? She was all right the last I seen. I swear she was." Brawley kept edging sideways, trying to peer past Longarm's shoulder at the bloody mess inside.

"When was the last time you looked in on her, Corporal?"

"I'd guess it was about the same time that you did, Marshal. She was asleep, just like you seen. Me, I was standing in the doorway at parade rest watching to make sure nobody tried to come in."

"She didn't try to get out?"

"No, sir. I never heard a peep outa her."

"Did anyone try to go in to speak with her?"

"No, sir. No one."

"Anyone look in at her?"

"No, sir." Brawley glanced at Sarah, who was standing nearby listening to Longarm's questions and the corporal's responses. "Nobody, sir."

Longarm thought Brawley looked just a little uncomfortable. Because of Sarah's presence?

"Sarah."

"Yes, Marshal?"

"I may need the mess hall for some more interrogation of the men. Would you please see to the kitchen crew? Ask them to speed things along if you would, please. Have them prepare something quick and easy so we can move breakfast along quickly."

Something, some emotion or other, flickered briefly in Sarah's eyes, but her facial expression betrayed nothing. The woman would be one helluva poker player, Longarm thought. If he were going to guess, it would be that Sarah thought she was above being ordered around. By anyone, much less by some white man who did not belong here.

"Please do it," George Haynes said to her, perhaps reading the reluctance in her posture. Or simply because he knew her well enough to anticipate her reactions. "It is important that we all cooperate with the marshal fully."

"Yes. Of course." Again Longarm got the impression she was gliding over top of the earth more than walking upon it.

When Sarah was gone, Longarm turned his attention back to Brawley. "You were about to say something, Corporal?"

"No, sir, I . . . well . . . yes. I mean, it's nothing. Nobody tried to go in and the girl never tried to come out."

"Did anyone come near? Try to look in perhaps? Try to reach her in any way?"

"No, sir. Not . . . exactly."

"What does that mean, Corporal?"

"It's Miss Sarah, sir. She never tried to go inside and she never came to the doorway to look in. But I seen her, um, standing over there sorta by the side of the building. She wasn't saying nothing exactly. She was singing. Real softlike. Not chanting. More like a regular song. But so soft I could scarce hear any of it. And she was doing, well, doing things, I dunno what. With her hands. Waving her arms around. Religious stuff, I figured. Injun religion, though, not like real religion. You know what I mean, sir?"

"Yes, of course. And she never went inside? Never called out to the girl in there?"

"No, sir. I'm pretty sure anybody inside wouldn't 've been able to hear what she was singing. And the girl was asleep anyhow. Was the last time I looked in, that is. I never heard her get up or roll around, and you know how those ropes creak and groan when you move around on them. I know, sir, because I generally sleep on that bed myself when I got off . . . uh, noncommissioned, that is, officer of the day duties." Brawley visibly shuddered. "I don't know as I'll want to sleep in there again, though. That's two women been killed there now. Spooky, that's what it is. I'm beginning to think that bed or that room or something is haunted, sir. Touched by ghosts and demons and like them."

Longarm frowned. Witchcraft? They said Sarah was a witch. Or what the whites would consider to be a witch. To an Indian she would more likely be considered a powerful medicine woman.

"Thank you, Brawley."

"Can I go now, sir?"

"In a minute. First I'd like you to take your shoes off."

"Sir?"

"Just take your shoes off. I want to get a look at them."

Brawley gave Longarm a look that said he thought the deputy was more than a little bit daft. But, first glancing at the lieutenant as if hoping for instruction, he bent and untied the heavy, clumsy, Army-issue shoes, then kicked them off and handed them to Longarm.

Longarm took them one by one, turned them over, and very closely examined the soles, even going to far as to scrape some of the accumulated grit away with a thumbnail.

Brawley looked puzzled at first. Then he relaxed. "I get it, sir. Blood. You're looking to see if I walked in all that blood in there."

"That's right, Corporal." Longarm smiled and returned the soldier's shoes to him. "Thank you for being so cooperative."

"I got nothing to hide, sir. I'm sorry for what happened in there, whatever the hell it was, but I didn't do it and for damn sure never knew anything about it."

"I believe you, Corporal."

Haynes nodded. "You are dismissed, Tom." The officer turned to Longarm. "Do you have any idea what happened, Long?"

"Maybe." Longarm took a final drag on his broken cheroot and dropped the butt in the dirt, grinding it out under the sole of his high-topped cavalry boot.

Haynes waited, standing in the doorway peering in at the dead girl and all the blood that surrounded her.

"I'm thinking she may've died from witchcraft, George."

Haynes immediately looked around in the direction Sarah had just gone. He shook his head. "No. That isn't . . . I am sure that is not possible. Really."

But the officer did not sound as if he believed his own protestations.

Longarm sighed. He wished to hell he understood just what the relationship was between George Haynes and that Indian medicine woman.

After a moment Longarm said, "That girl ain't going anywhere, George. I'd like you to put a guard on the door here. No one in an' no out. I'll come back an' finish up after breakfast. My belly is telling me it's past time for some grub."

104

Chapter 21

Longarm ate quickly, scarcely tasting the oat porridge and flapjacks that he stuffed down, then took a little more time to savor a cheroot and cup of coffee before he headed back to the lean-to where the dead girl awaited. He peered inside the small room and his expression registered distaste.

"Is anything wrong, sir?" the private who was guarding the door asked.

"Other than the obvious? Yeah. That blood is about half dry. It's stringy and gummy and it stinks. And I hafta go walking around in it. That's what is wrong, dammit."

"Would you like a suggestion, sir?"

"Of course."

"There's rubber boots in the stable. We keep them in the tack room just to the right of the door."

"Thanks." Longarm turned to walk over there, but the private stopped him with a polite "Sir?"

"Yes?" Longarm wished he could remember the young man's name but he could not.

"If you would relieve me here and watch the door for a

minute, I'd be glad to run over there and fetch them for you."

Longarm chuckled and asked, "Got to take a leak, do you?"

The soldier's grin was answer enough.

"All right. Go ahead then."

"You don't mind, sir?"

"Not at all."

The soldier saluted—unnecessary but polite—then dropped his rifle to port arms and double-timed to the stables. He was back within minutes looking much relieved and carrying a pair of gum-rubber boots in one hand, his Springfield rifle balanced in the other.

"Perfect. Thanks." Longarm kicked off his own boots and jammed his feet into the oversized rubber boots.

Even with the boots on he did not like walking through the half-dried blood. It felt slippery underfoot and clung like sticky mud. There was no other way in, however.

He was halfway through his examination of the girl's body when a slight reduction in the amount of light coming in through the open doorway told him someone was standing there.

"Yes, George?"

"Have you found out what killed her? Or who?"

Longarm nodded. "Yeah. Both."

Haynes raised an eyebrow. Another shadow moved beside the door. Longarm could not see who it was, but he suspected it would be the medicine woman Sarah moving closer so she could overhear what was being said.

"The girl killed herself," Longarm said. "With this." He held up a small sewing awl of the sort any Indian woman would be expected to carry on her person virtually all the time. The awl was made from the leg bone of some sort of bird, the bone deliberately splintered to a

106

fine point and further sharpened by rubbing it against a stone.

Longarm's guess that it was Sarah standing beside the door was confirmed. She peeped inside to see what he was showing to Haynes, then quickly withdrew as if she did not want Longarm to see that she was there.

"That doesn't look big enough to reach a vital organ," Haynes said, the tone of his voice skeptical.

"She didn't stab herself, George. She picked a vein open. A major artery actually. In the groin."

The lieutenant winced. "That must have hurt."

"Prob'ly hurt like hell," Longarm agreed, "but it was hell for effective. You can come in now if you want."

Haynes looked at the clotted, stinking mess on the floor and shook his head. "Not unless you need me in there for something."

"No. I'll be done here in a minute. I want t' make sure there's no other wounds."

"Such as?"

"Such as a lump on her head," Longarm said. "If she has a goose egg on her scalp, that'd suggest that somebody knocked her out. But I don't think I'm gonna find anything like that. Corporal Brawley said no one came in, and I see no reason to doubt the man."

"Brawley is a good man. Reliable," Haynes said.

"That's the impression I got too."

"Do you want me to assemble the men so you can talk with them again?" Haynes offered.

"No, thanks. There's no need. The girl committed suicide, and that's that. You can tell her people what happened. They can collect her body and bury her whenever they wish."

"What will you be doing?"

"The same thing I told you before. I'm gonna go out

an' look in on Many Thumbs and the Reverend Dascher."

"I thought . . . with another death on the post and everything . . ."

"I'm not needed here right now, George, an' I still have my orders. I'll look around out there an' then come back. Maybe I'll have some ideas then about what happened to Yellow Flowers at Sunrise."

"Yes, well, whatever you think best."

"I'll be going quick as I gather up my things."

Haynes nodded and turned away, motioning for the private who had been on guard duty to go with him. Sarah lingered only a moment, then followed leaving Longarm alone with the dead girl.

Chapter 22

Longarm scowled and reined his horse to a halt. The animal had begun limping quite badly, favoring its left foreleg and shaking its head. He slipped out of the saddle and passed the reins over the horse's head, holding onto them while he picked up the injured foot.

"Well . . . shit!" he mumbled aloud.

The animal seemed to have stepped on something—a scrap of hardwood buried in the ground or something of that nature—that became embedded deeply enough to cause the hoof to split. It was a lousy break and without an expert farrier's services, the only remedy would be to wait for the hoof to grow out past the point of the split.

There probably was no true farrier closer than Whitefish or possibly Kalispell, someone who could devise a walled shoe capable of holding the split together while accepting the weight of horse and rider, and it would take months of standing on soft tanbark in a closed stall to allow the hoof to grow out without further damage. Barring one of those remedies, the horse would be permanently ruined and might just as well be put down here and now.

Still, it did have a chance for survival. And Custis Long would have to hike back to Camp Converse and the Bright Star Reservation one way or the other. At least if he took the horse with him and put it into a stall there, it could carry his saddle and bedroll.

Longarm gently set the foot back onto the ground and tugged his pocketknife out. He opened the handy Barlow and picked the hoof up again. The horse snorted and tossed its head nervously.

"Steady, old son. This won't take but a minute."

Using the tip of the knife, he tried to pry the offending scrap of wood out. "Stubborn son of a bitch," he complained out loud, and tried once again to pop the wooden plug out of the hoof. Eventually, he had to cut away some of the broken hoof material and a little of the spongy frog as well in order to free the finger-thick plug.

The bit of wood fell free and Longarm once again set the foot down onto the ground. "I'd do more for you, boy, except I haven't any tools out here. Do we get you back to the barn, I'll make sure that foot is trimmed and tight wrapped." Musing aloud, he added, "I think I can take some green cowhide an' soak it so it will stretch, then sew it around the foot like a leather shoe. When it dries it'll be hard as steel, damn near. Should work to keep that hoof from getting any worse while you're standing around eating the post outa house an' home. What d'you think?"

The horse just stood there.

"Yeah. Maybe you're right. But I think it's worth a try."

Longarm took up the reins, and was about to begin leading the animal back the way he had just come when something on the ground caught his eye.

There was something about that stubby little piece of wood he had just removed from the hoof . . .

He bent and retrieved the object. "Well I'll be a green-haired son of a bitch," Longarm muttered as he examined the wood scrap.

A close look revealed that a knife had been used to whittle the wood for size and shape, then something hard and smooth, presumably a hammer, has been used on the other end to pound it into place.

It was, in effect, a wedge calculated to split the hoof after the weight of the horse stepping on that foot drove the wooden plug deeper.

Damn thing worked almighty well too.

Now the question was: Who the fuck would do such a thing? And perhaps even more important: Why?

Longarm was in a thoroughly shitty mood when he gently tugged on the reins and began walking the limping horse back toward Camp Converse.

"Back already? Good. I thought it would have taken you longer to find the preacher's camp and return."

Longarm was in no mood for long explanations or for socializing. He gave Haynes an explanation in the briefest terms and added, "I have authority from Washington to request a mount from your stables. It's almost dark now, too late t' be starting out again, but come morning I expect t' ride out of here on a fresh horse."

"I don't know that we have anything suitable," the lieutenant said. "The only decent mount available would be my own personally owned horse, and I'm not sure you have the authority to take him. I would have to check with company headquarters about that before I could allow it considering that the horse is not the property of the United States Government."

"Well, we damn sure ain't gonna take time for you to be writing letters back an' forth to some headquarters. If

111

you block me from using your horse, I'll just commandeer one from the Indians."

"Would that be legal?"

"If they want to object, fine. I'll take the horse an' use it. Then they can send letters back and forth afterward. Or you can do it for them." Longarm glanced toward the woman called Sarah, who seemed always to be somewhere close by. He was not sure how much of the conversation she understood, but she certainly was able to hear it. "What will it be, George? Should I put my saddle on your horse or on one of theirs?"

Haynes chuckled. "I am tempted to deny you permission, Long, just to see how one of those Indian ponies would react to a white man's saddle and bit. It could prove quite a show. Unfortunately, it would just create a lot of bother for everyone, so I suppose I must reluctantly give you permission to use my own mount. I want you to sign a paper, however, stating that you, or by extension the U.S. Attorney General, will be responsible for the health and well-being of my horse while you are using it."

"In case you need to lay a claim for recovery of damages?" Longarm asked.

"Well . . . yes, actually."

Longarm nodded. "Fair enough, George. I'll be leaving again at first light tomorrow. You want I should come by this evening to sign your paper?"

"No. It will take me some time to draw it up, and I have other things to attend to. I will have it on my desk in the morning. Meet me at post headquarters after breakfast."

"I'll be long gone from here by then."

"All right then, come by my quarters on your way out. If I am not awake come wake me. I will draw up the document before I sleep tonight. You can sign it first thing on the morrow and be on your way."

112

"Fine."

"Will you join me for dinner this evening, Long?"

"Thanks, but I don't think so. I'm just gonna grab a quick meal outa the mess hall an' find a place to bunk down." He made a sour face. "Not in that lean-to, though. It stinks of spilt blood in there. Reckon I can find a better spot than that to spread my blankets."

"I don't say as I blame you for that," Haynes said. "Very well then. I will expect to see you first thing in the morning. Now if you will please excuse me, I have duties to attend to."

Duties on this sad and dreary little post? Longarm wondered if the lieutenant's duties consisted of busting the cherry of some dusky little Indian maiden.

Not that it mattered, he supposed. One thing for sure was that George Haynes's duties were none of his business and none of his worry either. "Good night, George."

"Good night, Long."

Chapter 23

Longarm was vaguely uncomfortable being afoot in big country . . . and this most certainly was big country. When he left George Haynes outside the man's headquarters, he walked straightaway to the stables and first saw to the comfort of his original mount.

"He seems all right, sir. Well, pretty much so. Considering," said the private to whom Longarm had turned the animal over when he finally arrived back at the post.

"Now you'll remember what I told you about how to—"

The soldier cut him off with a grin and a stream of tobacco juice. "Go teach your mama to suck eggs, sir. I know how to doctor a hoof. I've already got a swatch of green cowhide soaking in a tub over there. When it's ready, I'll cut a piece to fit and sew it in place. Should wear like iron 'less he goes to walking in puddles or something."

"Right. Sorry," Longarm said.

"Was that all you wanted, sir? To check on your horse?"

"No, I'll also be needing Lieutenant Haynes's personal mount. He has been kind enough to give me the use of him for the time being."

The private looked surprised but said nothing.

"Use my saddle and gear, though, please."

"You'll be wanting him now, sir?"

"If you don't mind."

"Right away, sir." The soldier put down the broom that he had been needlessly pushing around an already clean dirt floor and hurried away to get the horse and Longarm's gear.

Five minutes later Longarm was mounted again. Five seconds after that he was unmounted.

And on his ass in the dirt.

"I should've mentioned to you, sir. He's a little bit fresh. The lieutenant don't ride him all that much."

"Thank you for that explanation." Longarm accepted the man's hand to help him to his feet. He brushed himself off and accepted the reins from the soldier . . . Albrecht, dammit, something-or-other Albrecht; that was the fellow's name. "Thank you very much, Private Albrecht."

He got back another grin.

This time Longarm was prepared when he swung into the saddle. And this time the bay horse acted like butter wouldn't melt in its mouth. It was docile as a lamb.

Longarm left the confines of the little post and headed up onto the ridge above it, in the opposite direction from the Indian encampment.

George Haynes's bay was a trifle small for Longarm's taste, but it had a smooth way of going and answered well to the rein, unlike some of the Remount Service cavalry horses that he'd found himself stuck with. Some of those had mouths like whang leather and brains of solid stone. This bay was a tolerable creature. Better, in fact, than he had expected of Haynes.

But then perhaps the lieutenant's ever-present shadow Snow Maiden had chosen it for him.

"Now I'm bein' catty as an over-the-hill whore," Longarm said aloud as he scratched the bay's poll. "Never mind."

He made quick work of putting a camp together, and sat in the gathering darkness looking down at the little Army post on the slope below. He was hungry, but the idea of going back down there where he was sure to be the center of attention . . .

Instead, he dug into his small bundle of trail rations and cobbled up a meal of jerky, hardtack, and skillet-boiled coffee. Trail fare indeed, but the truth was that it went down kinda good for a change. And his mood was definitely good a few minutes later when he spread his blankets and stretched out for an undisturbed sleep.

Longarm slept well on the hard ground, a condition he was certainly accustomed to, and woke early. A glance at the slow wheel of stars moving overhead suggested he had at least an hour to go before the sunrise.

He thought about preparing his own breakfast, but the lure of solid, hot mess hall chow was stronger. Stomach rumbling in anticipation of porridge and perhaps some bacon, he quickly broke camp and saddled the bay.

The horse was fractious at the early morning demand that it work for a living, but this time Longarm was prepared for its shenanigans and easily rode out a brief storm while the horse worked the kinks out of its spine. Once it was done fooling around, he pointed it downhill to the post where glowing windows and moving lights proved the garrison was awake and busy.

Longarm had not quite reached the camp when one of the soldiers came running out to meet him.

"Begging your pardon, sir, but you're needed. Real bad."

"What's wrong, soldier?"

"I . . . I best let the corporal tell you that, sir."

"Who . . . ?"

"Corporal Lassiter, sir," the private interrupted. "He's had us lookin' all over for you. I think you'll find him at headquarters, sir."

"All right, son, but can you tell me what's wrong?"

"I don't know as . . ."

Longarm hardened both his expression and his tone of voice. "That is an order, soldier."

"Yes, sir, I . . . it's the lieutenant, sir. Lieutenant Haynes."

"What about him?"

"The lieutenant seems . . . sir, he seems to've deserted."

"Jesus!" Longarm jabbed the bay in the flanks and headed for the headquarters building at a brisk lope.

Chapter 24

"The man can't have deserted, dammit. He's the post commander for God's sake."

"We can't find him, sir," Lassiter said. "He's never missed signing the morning report before, and he isn't in his quarters."

"Then could he be, um, visiting in some Indian girl's lodge?"

"He's never done anything like that before, sir."

"Well, the sun will be up soon. We can better look for him come daylight."

"Yes, sir."

"What about Sarah? Uh, Snow Maiden?"

"I haven't seen her, sir."

"Send a runner to the Indian encampment. Invite her to speak with me here. Or better yet, in the mess hall. I'll be there having something to eat."

"What about Lieutenant Haynes, sir?"

"I don't know of any indication there has been foul play nor that he would have abandoned his career and deserted. Sarah could well know where he is."

"Yes, sir. I'll send for her now, sir."

Longarm grumbled a little as he tied the bay to a rail beside the headquarters building and walked across the compound to the mess hall. Lights glowed through the windows there—as they did in nearly all the buildings on the post this morning—but the mess hall had the added inducement of mouth-watering scents drifting downwind of it too.

The Indian workers had food ready but no one to eat it, all the soldiers being engaged in the search for their commanding officer. Longarm helped himself to coffee and to generous portions of bacon—a little limp for his taste but mighty good nonetheless—along with rice and plenty of bacon gravy to pour over it. He chose a seat facing the doorway, but even so Sarah took him by surprise, coming in by way of the kitchen.

"You want me?"

Longarm looked the woman over. There were several different ways that question could be taken. He would have to answer in the affirmative to either of them. Sarah really was a fine-looking woman, and he couldn't help but have a reaction when she came and stood so close beside him that her nipples lightly brushed one ear and the back of his head. His pecker came up as strong and tall as a tent peg.

She had a faint, musky scent about her. Smoke and herbs and healthy woman flesh. Longarm breathed deep of it before he answered. "The troops are worried about George not being here. I thought you might know where he's gone."

"Why would I know this thing?"

"Because you are close to him and because you are very observant. Do you know where he is?"

120

"Where he is? No. What direction he go last night, yes. I see him leave his place."

"Was he alone?"

"Alo . . . oh. Was girl with him, you mean? No. No one is with him when he leave. Las' night he was still so very sorry about Mai who kill herself. He did not ask for girl to fuck-fuck."

"Do you know where he went then?"

"No."

"Was he on foot?"

"Yes, he was walk. You have his horse."

"Can you show me which direction he took?"

"I can show."

"Let me finish my breakfast then and I'll go with you." Longarm raised his voice. "Lassiter!"

"The corporal isn't here, sir. Can I help?"

"Thanks, Brawley. Yes, I expect that you can. I want you and Lassiter to call off the search for the lieutenant. Bring the men in for their breakfast and have them resume their duties as usual."

"Yes, sir." Brawley snapped a salute even though Longarm was a civilian and not entitled to that courtesy. The junior corporal executed a rigidly correct about-face and marched off into the pale light of an approaching dawn.

Chapter 25

As soon as Longarm was settled into the saddle, Sarah surprised him. She held a hand up for him to grasp, planted her foot on the toe of his left boot, and swung up onto the bay's broad butt immediately behind Longarm's cantle.

"This way," she said, leaning forward to extend an arm around his side and point. Her position made Longarm very acutely aware of the fact that this was one fine-looking woman, and he could feel the soft mounts of her breasts pressing tight against his back as she clung to him.

Clung, he thought, perhaps a little more tightly than might be strictly necessary for a woman who very likely grew up on and around horses.

Still, what the hell did Custis Long know about this woman? Or for that matter, about any woman? They were strange and foreign creatures each and every one.

But, um, interesting, he conceded.

"This way," he agreed, and put the horse into a slow walk that should not distress her just in case she proved to be nervous about riding with strange men on horseback.

Sarah took him up onto the ridge where he had camped the past night and had him turn west along it for a mile and a half or so.

"Wait," she said.

He drew rein and Sarah slid down to the ground. She bent over, and he could have sworn that he saw her nostrils flare. She reminded him of nothing so much as a hound coursing for scent. After a few minutes she snorted and came trotting back to Longarm and the bay.

Without speaking, she again stepped on his foot and swung up behind him. In the process of getting settled she must somehow have poked the bay in the flanks, because without warning the animal snorted and jumped forward.

Sarah cried out and wrapped herself around Longarm as tight as the skin on a sausage.

He could feel her pressed warm and soft against him. And could feel her arms wrapped around, her hands pressing against his belly.

Low on his belly.

Low on . . .

"Aw, shit," he mumbled.

Sarah's hands were not on his belly any longer. They were splayed wide and flat and pressing on his cock. Which was growing at quite an alarming rate.

He could feel a slight fluttering that . . . He laughed. And that was for damn sure what Sarah was doing too. She was wrapped around him tight as a tick sucking blood and she was laughing her pretty head off. It was the rippling in her belly and the shaking of her chest that he could feel back there.

Without him noticing—hardly—her busy and very clever fingers had already slipped the buttons of his fly open. Now she reached inside his britches, fumbled for the opening in his balbriggans, and pulled his cock out.

"Oh!" Her exclamation sent a puff of warm breath onto the back of his neck, and Sarah began to run her fingertips ever so gently up and down Longarm's by now quite fully erect shaft. "Big," she said.

"Hungry," he agreed.

"You want me?"

"Yes. I want you."

"Now?"

"Now," he said.

Without another word Sarah slid down off the horse again, and stood with her feet wide apart and hands on hips, her head tilted right prettily as she waited for him to step down and join her.

By the time Longarm got off the horse, Sarah was bare-ass naked. Her body fair took his breath away.

She was lean, with a flat belly and narrow chest that made her tits appear larger than they really were. She had nipples the size and color of small plums and a thick, black, curly bush.

"You like?" she asked.

Longarm's response was to take her in his arms and kiss her deeply. He bent, scooped her up with one arm behind her knees, and carried her to a reasonably level bed of fallen pine needles. Sarah smiled when he placed her gently down, her weight—and his when he lay down beside her—crushing some of the needles and bringing out their aroma.

The air was warm and the clouds immaculate. Somewhere nearby a jay complained about their intrusion into the solitude.

Sarah's fingers flew, quickly unbuttoning him and freeing him from his clothing.

"I like," she said when she saw the full size of him bumping up and down with the pulse of each heartbeat.

Longarm kissed her again, then cupped the back of her head and pressed her down toward his cock. Sarah drew back, resisting.

"Not in mouth, no."

Longarm raised an eyebrow. He was certainly not angry but he was mildly curious.

"Taboo," she said. "The spirits . . ." She paused, then shrugged and repeated, "Taboo."

"All right." Longarm smiled and kissed her. Her mouth was warm and tasted faintly of . . . licorice? Maybe. Whatever the flavor, she tasted fine, and her lips were soft and mobile.

When he explored inside the dark bush at her crotch, he found that she was dripping with the slippery, delightful juices of a mature woman. He kissed her nipples and suckled there for a spell while he continued to finger her, then let his tongue rove southward, into her navel and beyond.

"No." She stopped him when he reached the patch of black fur. "Taboo."

"For me too? All right." He kissed his way back up her torso and shifted on top of her.

Sarah opened herself to him. She reached between their bellies to take his shaft in her hand and guide him into the wet, heated depths of her body. She cried out once he was fully inside, and moved her hips slightly to better accommodate him.

When Longarm began stroking into her—slowly at first and then with increasing urgency—Sarah began a low, thrumming chant in a tongue Longarm was fairly sure he had never heard before. For damn sure he had no idea what she was saying.

But he knew mighty good and well what she was doing, and what Sarah was doing was fine. Just fine.

She rolled her belly and thrust hard against him to meet every thrust of his.

The sap built quickly and within a minute or so he knew he was going to explode within her.

For this first time.

After that . . . he smiled and nipped at the side of her neck with his lips . . . after that they would just have to see what happened.

Chapter 26

What happened was that Custis Long, deputy United States marshal, had met his match. And then some.

He purely wore himself out from humping and thrusting and driving the old tent pole deep into Snow Maiden's soft, wet middle.

His back ached from it all, and it was just a damned good thing that she was taking over on top, lying draped over him with her legs sprawled wide to ease his entry while she licked and nibbled at his nipples and back and forth across his chest.

Lordy, but this girl was fine! Eager and accomplished and receptive. Fine indeed. So good it didn't even bother him that she always stopped just short of licking or sucking his cock. Taboo, she'd said. That was all right. She did not in the least mind sucking his balls and licking his ass. And she had so much muscle control in her pussy that it felt like she had a third hand down there whenever he slipped inside her . . . and that was plenty often and plenty enjoyable.

Longarm opened his eyes and peered upward through the dark lace of pine limbs.

"It's past noon. Are you getting hungry?"

Sarah stopped what she was doing long enough to lift her pretty head and nod. "I am hungry, yes."

"Yeah, me too. You think we should go back to the post?"

"Soon. Let me have you one more time."

They'd been at it so hard and so frequently already that his pecker was red and sore. Not that it stopped him. Sarah's touch brought him erect again—perhaps not quite so quickly as the first few times—and she slid down over him, the heat of her body enveloping and soothing him.

"Nice," he said.

Sarah said nothing in return. But then she did not have to. She closed her eyes and grunted with effort. After a very brief few moments she screamed, her climax loud and lusty, then collapsed on top of Longarm. He was not quite finished yet, but a few slow strokes into the unconscious woman's body took care of that.

He was fairly sure he did not have a drop of semen left anywhere in him, but the sensation was as powerful as if he had a quart to get rid of. Longarm grunted with pleasure, then let his hips down. Sarah slept on, her face lying in the hollow of his throat, the warmth of her sheath still holding onto his cock.

She lay like that for not more than three or four minutes—but pleasant minutes, very pleasant—before she roused herself and kissed him as she lifted herself away from him, his cock sliding out of her body and feeling almost chill when the air again reached it.

"It is late," she said.

"Not too late."

"I ask you one question, yes?"

"Yes, of course." Longarm sat up and reached for the coat he had discarded several hours earlier. He badly wanted a smoke now. And some lunch wouldn't be bad either.

"You say we come look for lieutenan'. Why we not look?"

Longarm smiled. "Because George has no more run away than I have." He bit the twist off the tip of a cheroot and struck a match to light it. The smoke tasted wonderfully rich.

"Why you say this?"

"For one thing, he is on foot. He could have taken the horse. It belongs to him, after all. But he didn't. And anyway, George is not the sort of man to desert."

"You do not think he run away?"

"No, I don't."

"Then why you look for him?"

"I was supposed to sign a paper for him, something about my using his horse for official government purposes. He insisted that it had to be done, and I don't think it's something he would have forgotten. So something came up that was more important to him. Could be something as simple as a woman. I don't know. But I figure to find out when George comes back from wherever he is. In any case, I don't think he's run away or even lost. Wherever he is and whatever he's doing, it's on purpose."

"And when you come out here with me?"

He laughed again and reached over to stroke her breast and gently squeeze her tit.

"You know I will fuck with you?" she asked.

"I didn't know. But I hoped you would."

"I do not fuck with the lieutenan'," she said.

"I kinda thought that you didn't. Why is that?"

"Lieutenan', if he have a woman he think he own her. Think she ignorant little red toy. You know what I mean?"

"Yes, I expect that I do, Snow Maiden."

"I think you are not this way." She giggled, and Longarm raised an eyebrow.

"The lieutenan'," she said. "He think I am virgin."

"I promise I won't give away your secret then." Longarm stuck the cheroot between his teeth and reached for his clothing. He did not bother to drag out his trusty old Ingersol pocket watch, but judging from the position of the sun he guessed it was somewhere around one in the afternoon. "Let's go back and see if George has showed up by now."

Sarah smiled and bounced to her feet. She was pretty as a picture when she leaned down to pick up her dress. "You go alone. I must . . . there are things I must do now. Prayers to offer."

"All right."

Sarah slipped the dress over her head, fluffed her hair with a shake of her pretty head, and stepped into her moccasins.

Without a word or a look back, she turned and ran down the slope toward the distant Indian encampments. Her movements were as graceful and lithe as a deer, and Longarm stood watching her until she was out of sight. Then he dropped his cigar butt to the ground and carefully crushed it with the toe of his boot before he took up the reins of the bay horse and swung into the saddle for the ride back to Camp Converse.

"Did you find him, sir?" Lassiter came running to ask as soon as Longarm entered the compound.

"He isn't back yet? Damn. I thought sure he'd be back by now."

"Sir?"

"The lieutenant has not deserted, Corporal. I'm sure of that. Whatever he is up to, he has not abandoned his post."

"Are you sure of that, sir?"

"Pretty sure, yes."

The corporal turned his head and barked, "Private! Front and center."

A soldier who had been walking nearby stiffened and came hurrying over at that odd, ramrod-up-the-ass gait that the Army teaches to its people. "Yes, Corporal."

"Take the gentleman's horse. Bathe and groom it and clean the tack before you put it away."

Longarm stepped down from the saddle and turned the borrowed horse over to the private—Hassan was the man's name as he recalled from the interrogations after Mai was killed—then walked with Lassiter back toward the headquarters building.

"You'll be staying over another day, sir?" Lassiter asked. Longarm noticed that the corporal was walking normally now, not in the approved stiff and unnatural military manner.

"I suppose I'll have to," Longarm told him. "I'm supposed to sign that damned paper for the lieutenant."

"Yes, sir. That's very important to him, I know."

"Why?"

Lassiter shrugged. "Damn if I know, sir. The lieutenant, he ain't usually such a stickler for paperwork. Most ways he's pretty easygoing. That's the one thing as makes this place bearable."

"That and the Indian girls from the camp over there," Longarm said with a grin.

Lassiter's face widened into a slow grin of his own. "Why, sir, I don't be knowin' what the gentleman could be sayin'."

"I am sure you don't, Corporal."

"Shall I tell the cook to expect you for supper, sir?"

Longarm glanced up toward the sky. The day was getting away from him, "Yes, I suppose so. But only for tonight. I'm leaving tomorrow morning with or without the lieutenant's damn paper."

"Yes, sir. I will see that your horse . . . the lieutenant's horse, I mean . . . I'll see that it's ready before first light, sir." Lassiter stopped, stiffened, and saluted.

"Thank you, Corporal." Longarm tossed a salute back at the man before he consciously realized he was going to do it. It was a breach of protocol since he was long since out of uniform himself, but there had been a time in his life when that response was as automatic as breathing.

Lassiter went double-timing on about his duties while Longarm headed inside headquarters to wait for that annoying damned lieutenant.

Chapter 27

"Wait, Custis Long. Wait for me one minute."

"Yes, Snow Maiden?" he asked, halting his long stride and turning back to face her. She'd caught him crossing the compound after supper on his way to the stables where he intended to bunk down for the night. He damn sure was not going back to the blood-sodden lean-to beside the headquarters.

"You will leave us in the morning?"

"How did you hear that?"

She shrugged. "The ladies in kitchen. Soldiers talk. They hear. Sometime they talk about. I hear."

"It's true enough. I expect to be on the way before first light tomorra."

"But what about lieutenan'? What about this paper you must sign for use horse?"

"I've waited as a courtesy. It isn't a requirement. He knew I wanted to get away and he's chosen to go traipsing off after some girl. His choice, not mine, and his privilege to do so, but I ain't gonna wait around for him to wear himself out. I just want t' go see the reverend so I can get my duty done with an' get back to my boss in Denver." Get back to other things in Denver too, of course, but that was none of Snow Maiden's never-mind.

Sarah stepped closer. She tipped her chin down and looked up at him with her eyes wide in that coquettish way that all women seem to know regardless of their race or culture. She reached up and toyed with a button on his shirt. "I thought . . . tomorrow . . . we could . . . you know . . ."

"You know there's nothing I'd like better, Snow Maiden, but I hafta get my work done. We can play some more you an' me when I bring George's horse back to him. Fact is, we'll prob'ly have lots of time to play like that. I'll need a ride back to the fort so's I can requisition another horse. It could be a while before there's a wagon or a coach headed that way for me to ride with. We'll have lots o' time then."

Sarah fashioned a pout. "But I make nice plans for to-morrow, Custis Long."

He smiled and leaned forward to plant a light kiss on her forehead. "Sorry, but I hafta go soon as I get around in the morning. I'll see you when I get back from the reverend's camp meeting."

Despite the fact that they were standing in plain sight in the Camp Converse compound, Sarah reached down to fondle his cock through his britches while her tongue wandered across the base of his throat. Longarm discovered that he might not be as completely worn out as he'd thought he was earlier in the day.

"If you stay," she whispered, "I teach you something new."

"Good. Wonderful. But why wait. We can slip over to the stables right now an' . . ."

"Not now. I must do . . . there are things I must do now. For my people. Tomorrow I teach."

"When I get back then, dear girl. I can't put off my duty any longer. I gave George today an' he missed his chance for getting that signature he wanted. Fine. Tomorra morning I'm leaving with or without it." He kissed her gently. "And you can count on the fact that I'll be hurrying t' get back here, girl."

"Then go. I cannot stop." She turned and hurried off into the gray dusk.

Longarm watched her out of sight, one very pretty Indian woman who was approaching middle age but had lost none of her beauty nor her natural charm. It was hard to believe that a pretty woman like that could have such power as a medicine woman that she would dominate all the disparate tribes of this thrown-together Indian encampment.

It occurred to him that he did not in fact know just which tribe Snow Maiden belonged to.

Not that it mattered.

He headed for the sinks to take an overdue crap, then back to the stables, where he spread his bedroll and turned in for the night.

Longarm was awake before reveille. He sat up stretching and yawning and took his time about standing upright. He was not on any sort of schedule, but he did intend this time to go find that damned revival site so he could take a look at what the Reverend Dascher was up to and report back to Billy Vail.

This time. For some reason that small train of thought caught his attention.

It was true. Every time he tried to head out to

Dascher's revival, something happened to delay him. He wondered if . . . no. Surely not. He shook his head and belched, then stepped into a nearby stall and pissed in the corner for that always welcome early morning relief.

He was busy tidying his bedroll into a neat cylinder so he could tie it when one of the garrison's soldiers came running in.

"Sir." The soldier stopped and gulped for breath. "You got . . . to come . . . sir. There's . . . trouble."

"What sort of trouble, Waverly?" Longarm hoped he had the name right.

"The lieutenant, sir."

"What about him?"

"He's . . . he's dead, sir." The hesitation in Waverly's voice this time was not the want of air but the enormity of the news he was sent to convey. "Lieutenant, Haynes has been murdered, sir."

"Tell me." Longarm was already reaching for his coat and hat and buttoning his vest. The .44-caliber Colt already rode in its accustomed place at his belly.

"The Corporal of the Guard went into the lieutenant's quarters with a mind to wake him, sir. At reveille, you see. Sometimes the lieutenant don't want to get up, see, but regulation says that he's to be notified so we always done that. Except this morning when Brawley went to wake him, he found the lieutenant stone dead."

"Do you know how he died?"

"No, sir, I surely don't. But the lieutenant, he's the only officer we got. Or did have, I expect I should say now. So we thought . . . you being an officer of the government and all . . . we thought we should report this to you, sir."

"You did the right thing," Longarm said, tugging his Stetson into place. "Take me to him if you please, Waverly."

"Yes, sir, right away, sir." The soldier snapped to attention and saluted.

This time Longarm felt no awkwardness when he returned the salute.

Waverly was right. He *was* the only officer of the United States Government present on this military reservation at the moment.

Chapter 28

George Haynes's quarters stank. Longarm was not usually so sensitive to such things, but at this early hour and with no forewarning, he felt his gorge rise and his gut tighten the moment he walked into the lieutenant's tiny, very spartan bedroom. It was no wonder Brawley was standing guard from outside the room.

"Nobody touched anything, sir," Brawley called from well beyond the doorway.

"Good. Thanks." Longarm stopped to light a cheroot, hoping that would help mask some of the stench.

George Haynes had been a tidy man when it came to his person. He would have been embarrassed to have been found in this state.

Haynes was naked, lying spread-eagled on his back in the center of his bed. The bed was wide enough for two. But then George was a man who had liked his overnight company.

Now he lay with his arms flung wide and his disbelieving eyes open.

What appeared to be a standard-issue bayonet had

been driven through his heart and completely through his body so that only the attaching socket was visible above Haynes's pale, scrawny chest.

Haynes had had no chest hair. None at all. Longarm fixated on that, trying to avoid thinking about the mess Haynes had made when he died. Both his bladder and his sphincter had voided so that the Army-issue blanket beneath the body was soaked with piss and heavy with the man's shit.

There was another scent hanging faint and barely detectable in the room, but Longarm could not figure out what it was, and after a moment inside the bedroom his senses closed down and he was no longer able to smell anything other than the lieutenant's evacuations.

With the cheroot between his teeth, Longarm went to the lieutenant's side and gave a closer look at the body.

There were no marks to indicate Haynes had been tied down. But there were indications on the corner posts of his bed suggesting that he had been known to tie his overnight visitors in the same position he now was himself.

Retribution from one of the girls he had kept in here? Longarm wondered. From the girl or someone in her family? Possible, he supposed, if unlikely. Whatever Haynes liked to do in here, Longarm had no reason to think it was not consensual. And the young Indian girls, not knowing anything about the white man's habits or culture, would have accepted as normal nearly anything Haynes liked to do with them.

Longarm tilted his head to keep the smoke out of his eyes and continued peering at the body. He was becoming inured to the stink and it no longer bothered him quite so much now.

No rope marks on wrists or ankles, he saw, and no scrapes or other suggestions of violence on the man's

142

knuckles or in his palms. He had not fought with his killer, nor had he tried to fend away or to grasp the long sliver of steel that drove into his chest.

Perhaps he had been asleep? Longarm went back to the doorway.

"Were you the one who found him?" he asked the corporal there.

"Yes, sir. When I come to wake him."

"Was there a lamp burning at the time?"

"Why . . . now that you mention it, sir, there was. That same one on the chest of drawers there. The wick was turned down real low . . . I turned it up higher so I could see better . . . but when I got here it was burning real low. Like . . . well, like the lieutenant wanted it trimmed when he was having one of his girls in. The lieutenant, he liked to see 'em. If you know what I mean, sir."

"And his clothing. Did you pick anything up?"

"No, sir. Everything was just exactly like you see it now. His stuff was all hung up nice an' tidy or put away somewhere."

"What time did Lieutenant Haynes return to the post last night?"

"I didn't mark down the exact time or anything, but I'd say it was a little before midnight."

"Was he alone?"

"Yes, sir, but he was expecting company."

"How do you know that? Did he tell you?"

"Oh, he wouldn't say nothing like that to any of us enlisteds, sir, but all the signs was there. He had me fetch a jar of hot water from the mess hall. He had his razors and brushes and stuff laid out ready to shave and get himself cleaned up when I brought the water. Like, well, like he usually done when he had a girl with him."

The shaving gear was not on display now and—

Longarm looked again—Haynes was freshly shaved. He had had time enough to finish grooming and put everything away again.

"But he was alone at the time?" Longarm asked.

"Yes, sir."

"Did he give any indication of who he was expecting?"

"No, sir, he didn't."

"Did you see anyone join him?"

"No, sir, but then the Corporal o' the Guard stays overnight in headquarters. You can see the commanding officer's quarters from there if you like, but there wasn't no reason to pay attention to this building. I mean, of course there was a reason. But I didn't know it at the time. I never seen whoever it was that the lieutenant had come in."

"So it could have been anyone. Or any number of people."

"Yes, sir, it could've been."

Longarm sighed. "All right. Thank you, Brawley."

The corporal turned away, and Longarm went back to his examination of the dead man.

There were no lumps anywhere on his scalp to suggest that he had been knocked out, which would have explained why he put up no defense against his killer. Yet he had not offered resistance, at least nothing that Longarm could see now.

Longarm sniffed his palms after he checked Haynes's scalp. There was a lingering scent of hair tonic. Longarm could not remember the brand, but he was sure he had smelled it before.

He stood for a time looking down at the dead man. The dark bayonet socket looked odd there, sprouting from the center of George Haynes's chest.

Haynes had not been all that large a man to begin with, and in death he was diminished so that now there was little to him except unnaturally pale flesh and a little bone.

In life he had been a randy little bastard. Now his pecker was shriveled up and drawn back inside his body so that all that was visible was the pinkish purple tip. He had been circumcised, something that Longarm happened to know often fascinated and sometimes delighted dusky Indian maidens.

Not that any of this helped, dammit.

Longarm spun away from the dead man and strode into the outer room. "Do you have an ice house, Brawley?"

"No, sir. I mean, well, yes, sir, we do. But there's no ice in it. We didn't cut none last winter. The lieutenant didn't want to bother. He's been using it as the garrison jail instead."

"So much for trying to preserve the body until higher authority can be contacted. All right then, have the men turn out. We will have no choice but to bury him here. Give me a work detail . . . after breakfast . . . to prepare the grave. We'll have the entire garrison present for the burial later this morning."

"Very well, sir." There was no hint of resistance to a stranger, and not even an Army officer at that, taking charge. If anything, Brawley seemed relieved that Longarm was assuming command of the situation.

"And I will want your best horseman, Corporal. Someone who knows the way to higher headquarters. I want to send a dispatch telling them about the situation here."

"Right away, sir." Brawley saluted, waited for Longarm to return it, then spun on his heels and hurried away to start getting things done.

Longarm glanced into the bedroom one more time, by now hardly mindful of the smells. He shook his head.

"Shit!" he blurted aloud into the empty room.

Chapter 29

"Ready. . . . Aim. . . . *Fire*!   Ready. . . . Aim. . . . *Fire*!
Ready. . . . Aim. . . . *Fire*!" Corporal Lassiter barked the
orders and his squad responded, firing into the air at his
command while Brawley and his squad froze in place at
"Present Arms."

Longarm hadn't been sure exactly how many volleys
of rifle fire would be appropriate, so he had Lassiter's
squad fire in unison three times as the send-off for Lieutenant George Haynes. Longarm marched forward to order the garrison, the pitifully few men who comprised
that body, into lines facing the empty grave.

On Longarm's signal, six of the enlisted men stepped
one pace forward to take up the ropes that cradled the
coffin. They lifted and two other men slid away the
planks that held the wooden box above ground.

"Ready," Lassiter murmured in a low, deep voice.
"Down."

The coffin was lowered, not all that gently but lowered, into the earth.

Longarm did not know what the hell to say about

147

Haynes so he settled for reading from a Bible he'd found in the lieutenant's quarters. When he was done with that, he took a step back and nodded to Lassiter, who had the men, already standing at rigid attention, present arms again. Then the senior corporal shouted, "Dis . . . missed," and the little formation dissolved. Two privates remained behind to fill in the grave, the work detail obviously assigned to them ahead of time.

"Do you have that dispatch ready, sir?" Lassiter asked as they walked downhill toward the camp.

"All set for your rider, corporal."

"Sir."

"Yes?"

"You know that we don't have a horse for him, don't you? There's just your animal . . . but he's hobbled by that bad hoof. And the lieutenant's horse, but you are using him. The supply wagon is a couple days overdue or I'd say we could use one of the wagon horses. What shall I tell the dispatch rider, sir?"

"Have him take the lieutenant's bay. It's a good horse."

"Very well, sir. Thank you, sir."

Longarm heard the pounding of hoofs on turf within fifteen minutes or so, even before he could complete the chore of repacking his gear, separating his few things into two bundles, one of which was small, light, and very tightly wrapped.

"Lassiter!" he called.

The corporal quickly stepped to the headquarters doorway. "Sir?"

Longarm picked up the smaller bundle and slung it over his shoulder by the latigo he had used to secure it. "I'll be gone for a while, Corporal. Could be for as much as a couple days. I'm not sure how long I will be. In the meantime you are in charge of the post."

"Do you think that's a good idea, sir? You're the only officer we got now."

"Corporal, I am not an officer in the United States Army."

"Yeah, I know, sir, but . . . you know what I mean."

"I won't be all that long, Corporal. You can handle things here I'm sure."

"What about the Injuns, sir?"

"I will tell them what the situation is here." Longarm grinned. "I kind of have to since I need to borrow a horse from them."

Lassiter looked worried, but he offered no more objections. He stepped respectfully aside when Longarm strode briskly toward the door, determined that this time he was damned well going to find the Reverend Samuel Dascher's revival meeting and take a look at what was going on there.

It could not possibly be coincidence, Longarm figured, that every time he said he was going out to that camp some dire new event occurred here on the military post to prevent his leaving.

Well, not this time, dammit.

George Haynes was dead. Those two Indian girls were dead. Nothing he could accomplish here would bring either of them back.

But it was just possible that a visit to the revival meeting might help him understand why those people died.

He intended to borrow a pony from John Apple and his Indians . . . or commandeer one if it came to that.

But come hell or high water, he *was* riding out to find the Reverend Dascher. And he was going to do it today.

Chapter 30

Whatever was going on here, Longarm believed, pretty much had to be coming from within the Indian community, and after three deaths and a deliberately injured horse, he had to believe that someone over there did not want him to find that revival camp.

God knows—literally, he supposed—what sort of twisted reasoning lay behind that sequence of events, but he was convinced now that there was a deliberate campaign under way to keep him away from the Reverend J. Samuel Dascher and his tent meeting.

It seemed crazy, but it was the only logical conclusion he could think of. If it were true, then the last thing he wanted to do was to let John Apple and Snow Maiden and the rest of the Indian leadership know what his intentions were now.

He was supposed to be concentrating on running Camp Converse. Let them assume that he was doing exactly that.

After telling Lassiter that he intended to borrow a horse from John Apple, Longarm changed his mind.

He stole one instead.

It was not exactly difficult. He slung his own headstall and bit over his shoulder and walked away into the hills, circling around the Indian encampment and walking in plain sight into the herd of ponies.

A pair of half-grown boys were engaged in some sort of game—on a hillside overlooking the herd. Longarm waved to them and got a friendly wave in return.

He picked out a sleek, seal-brown gelding that still had cinch marks on its belly and dollar-sized white patches of hair where saddle sores once healed over. Likely the brown was raised and broken to saddle by some white rancher, then either bought or stolen to end up here in the hills of Montana Territory.

However it came to be here, it was Longarm's clear choice for a mount since it was the least likely of these ponies to resist his use of a metal snaffle bit, Indians generally preferring to use only a bosal or even a single thong tied around the jaw. And they seldom used saddles. Longarm had no intention of heading deeper into the hills riding bareback. His ass would never forgive him if he were to do a thing like that.

The brown let him approach as readily as the herd guards did, and he first put an arm over the horse's neck, then slipped the headstall into place. The brown took the sweet copper bit with no resistance.

"Attaboy," Longarm muttered, arranging the reins and springing onto the brown's back. He wriggled around enough to be sure of his seat, then squeezed the horse into an easy walk.

He headed back to Camp Converse so he could pick up his saddle and get on about the business that someone seemed determined to thwart.

• • •

Finding the revival proved to be far easier than Longarm had expected. The route leading to it had been used often enough and by enough people that it was practically a road. Certainly it was a trail that was easy to follow.

Longarm set the brown onto the path and loped right along. He would have had to admit to a feeling of some relief when he got past the point where his horse came up lame on his last attempt.

But then this time no one else knew where he was going, and the brown was freshly stolen so no one could possibly have known he would be riding it.

Keeping him away from the revival seemed to have been worth three lives to someone, but he doubted that the culprit would have thought to injure every horse in the Indians' herd, never mind if they would have been willing.

Three lives. Longarm persisted in thinking that the young woman who committed suicide—and she had indeed done exactly that as his very own investigation showed—even though her death truly was by her own hand, he had to believe that it was part and parcel of this insistence that he not learn what was happening at the revival.

His suspicion quite frankly was that J. Samuel Dascher was a charlatan, no more a Bible-pounding, Gospel-quoting tent preacher than Longarm was.

Dascher and that son-of-a-bitch renegade Many Thumbs were up to something.

And Custis Long intended to prove it.

Chapter 31

Samuel Dascher's revival was set up in about as pretty a little valley as Longarm could remember seeing anywhere. A sparkling clear creek meandered down the length of it, punctuated by a string of ponds backed up above beaver dams. It looked like a place where a man could find true relaxation catching trout out of the creek and watching his ponies grow fat on the lush grass that grew in the bottom.

Stands of quakies were scattered over the hillsides above the creek, and there were berry patches to attract black bears while herds of deer likely grazed here most of the time.

Most of the time. Not now.

Now the beauty of the valley was marred by the smoke from a dozen fires, and brush arbors had been erected to house the crowd of fifty or so Indians Longarm could see from the hillside where he lay on his belly to observe the situation.

The emerald grass was trampled and muddy at this

point, and what was not trampled had been mostly eaten by the herd of horses that grazed outside the camp.

The central focus of this arrangement was a large circular tent, the side walls rolled up now to allow air to flow through. The big tent had alternating orange and red panels of canvas. Longarm's guess was that the Reverend Dascher had saved a little money by buying his tent secondhand from a circus. Longarm halfway expected to see some elephants nearby.

Come to think of it, a couple elephants would likely be a fine idea for a tent meeting aimed at drawing in a bunch of Indians. They would have been damned well fascinated.

Longarm lay behind the bole of a particularly large aspen and chewed on some jerky and a cold biscuit while he waited for things to heat up down below. Apparently the Reverend Dascher liked to do his preaching in the evenings—if in fact the man did any preaching—or possibly the camp was just taking a siesta after a hard morning of listening.

There was no sign of Samuel Dascher that Longarm could see. There were plenty of Indians in view, but no activity to speak of. Most seemed either to be smoking, sleeping, or playing at one game or another.

One thing Longarm was sure of. If these people were up to something they oughtn't to be, they were not going to show him what it was if he just walked in and looked around. His best bet, he realized, was simply to wait here and see what happened.

His wait was rewarded just as the sun was setting. The light was dim enough that he could not see clearly for any great distance, but he could make out some sort of commotion among the horses at the far upper end of the valley. A short while later, one Indian separated himself from the others and walked up in that direction, only to return a few minutes later with a newcomer to the camp.

Longarm unbuckled his saddlebags and found his field glasses. He grunted once he got them in focus and trained on the pair who were entering the camp.

Many Thumbs. And Snow Maiden.

Had Sarah come to warn Many Thumbs and Dascher about Longarm? Unlikely, he decided. She had no way to know he had a horse or that he had come to join the crowd here at the Reverend Dascher's tent.

He lay where he was and watched the way the other Indians in the camp reacted to Sarah.

Except now, it was plain enough to see, this was not Sarah; this was Snow Maiden, a powerful and feared medicine woman. A sorceress. A witch.

Longarm was not so sure about all of that. But it was plain that these Indian warriors respected her. Hell, the way they acted, pulling back so that her shadow did not pass across them when she walked by, they were probably afraid of her.

All except for Many Thumbs.

Many Thumbs the meek and gentle Christian convert, Longarm reminded himself. Or so he was told.

Yeah. Sure. Not that this would be a bad thing. Far from it. But Longarm couldn't help but be skeptical. The son of a bitch.

After more than an hour spent on the hilltop watching the camp, the activity down there began to change.

A tall white man wearing a cutaway and top hat emerged from one of the arbors and began giving orders by way of gestures, assigning small tasks to a number of the nearby Indians.

Lanterns were produced and hung around the circumference of the tent, and the men—all of them male, Longarm noticed now—began to slowly gather beneath the red and orange canvas panels.

It was almost completely dark now.

Dascher and his converts all went inside the tent.

Longarm carefully packed his field glasses away and carried his saddlebags to the brown horse, which was tied to the trunk of a tree. He strapped the bags in place, then drew the cinches on his old McClellan snug.

"Sorry t' be leaving you like this, old son, but it's possible you an' me could be leaving here in one helluva hurry." He rubbed the horse's poll and added, "Better you should be uncomfortable, y'see, than I should be shot for bein' too slow leaving outa here. But I tell you what. When we get back t' the post I'll double your grain ration, how's that."

He looked for a moment at the carbine in its boot under the stirrup fender, then decided against taking the long gun with him. There were sixty or seventy Indians inside that tent down there. If he managed to piss them off, he would need more than a Winchester to get him out of the jam.

"I'll be back," he said to the horse, taking the optimistic view of things.

Then he started easing very slowly and quietly down toward the revival tent where the Reverend J. Samuel Dascher's fine baritone voice was commencing to float out onto the night air.

Chapter 32

Longarm crawled the last couple rods on his belly, heart pounding, sheer determination turning his expression to granite. Staying in the shadows, he crept close to the line of tent poles behind the raised platform where Dascher was standing, voice raised and hands gesturing wildly to emphasize this point or that one.

A pair of parfleches, each the size of a small steamer trunk, provided cover for Longarm to lie behind. He was fairly sure no one inside the tent would be able to see him there in deep shadow.

At least he damn well hoped he could not be seen.

He wriggled sideways until he could put an eye to the gap between the parfleches. He could see the back of J. Samuel Dascher's head and the man's upper shoulders. An Indian stood close beside him. Dascher would reel off a string of exhortations, then pause while the Indian translated for the benefit of those who had no English.

"The Lord is just," Dascher shouted. "The Lord is merciful."

Yuk-yuk-yuk, the fellow beside him translated.

"His mercy knows no bounds."

Yuk-yuk-takpa.

Longarm stiffened. Blinked. Except . . . no. He couldn't have heard that correctly. He was just imagining things.

"Come to Jesus," Dascher shouted.

Yuk-*takpa*-yuk. Maybe he had heard correctly, dammit.

The tent full of worshippers erupted into shouts of approval and joy.

Dascher was encouraged by the support of his native congregation. His voice rose to a higher pitch and he shouted, "Come, brothers, come!"

"Yuk-*takpa*-yuk-yuk-*wakte*-yuk." The crowd went wild with approval.

Dascher was joyous.

Longarm was sick to his stomach.

He did not speak any of the several languages that were common among these tribes, but over the years he had picked up a few isolated words here and there. Among them were a few words in the Lakota tongue.

Takpa, for instance. And *wakte*.

Takpa was the Lakota word for "attack." *Wakte* meant "killing" or "kill," he was not exactly sure which was closer.

Dascher was up there speaking earnestly about mercy and justice.

The translator was speaking about an attack that would lead to an orgy of killing.

And it was the translator's version that was drawing the roars of happy approval.

Dascher held his arms up, palms out, and waited for the crowd to become silent.

"I have a special treat for you tonight," he said loudly. "Our brother in Christ, Many Thumbs, has agreed to give his first sermon this evening. Many Thumbs, my dear brother, come. Come and speak to your people."

Longarm's blood ran cold when he saw that murderous son of a bitch step onto the platform.

Many Thumbs was not painted for war. Not yet. But he had lost none of the arrogant cockiness that Longarm remembered from the last time they met.

The familiar necklace of human bone hung on his chest like a medieval breastplate, the thumb bones yellowing now with age.

The man had a pair of eagle feathers skewering a thick rope of hair much like a white woman would use hairpins to hold her bun together. The tips of Many Thumbs's feathers pointed downward and lightly brushed his massive shoulders.

He was one big son of a bitch, heavily muscled and oiled with some sort of grease so the sharp definition of his muscle tone stood out clearly in the lamplight inside the tent.

Many Thumbs ignored the Reverend Dascher, strutting and preening in the glow of admiration from his people.

He went to the dais and held up his arms for silence. The crowd immediately went quiet, and Many Thumbs began to speak. Again Longarm was sure he caught mention of the word *takpa*, and also the Lakota word for gun, which was *maza . . . maza*-something. *Mazawaka*, Longarm thought.

Guns. Attacks. Killing!

Samuel Dascher was preaching the Gospel.

Many Thumbs was very openly and with Dascher's help planning insurrection.

"Jesus!" Longarm muttered under his breath. He wondered if . . .

His train of thought was lost when he saw Many Thumbs motion toward someone at the back of the tent. The crowd went instantly silent, and a moment later the medicine woman Snow Maiden stepped onto the platform to join Many Thumbs and the Reverend Dascher there.

The question in Longarm's mind now was whether he could trust these red bastards to stay put here in the wilderness while he ran to bring help. And if the pitiful handful of soldiers who were there, with no officer to lead them, would do any good even if he did convince them of the need to come here.

That question was answered with a sudden roar from the crowd and the rumble of wagon wheels from the lower end of the valley.

Chapter 33

Warriors came boiling out of the tent like so many quail kicked off a nest. Fortunately for Longarm, they were going the opposite direction.

Poor Reverend Dascher was left standing alone and dumbfounded on his platform. He was obviously even more confused than Longarm about all of this.

The confusion was beginning to clear to some small extent anyway, Longarm thought. He had been dead wrong about Samuel Dascher and Many Thumbs being in cahoots about whatever it was that was going on in this valley. Obviously, Many Thumbs had gulled the preacher into being an unwitting dupe in whatever game Many Thumbs and his murderers were playing.

Probably, Longarm guessed, the Indians needed a pretext that would allow them to assemble a war party—and that was exactly what this was because the "worshippers" here were every one of them men—out from under the watchful eyes of the United States Army.

The sound of a wagon coming in and their instant

abandonment of Dascher suggested that the plan was coming together now and the old preacher was no longer needed by Many Thumbs and his renegades.

As for Snow Maiden, she was the spiritual leader of these Indians, and might hold temporal power over them as well. Neither John Apple nor Many Thumbs was suitable to serve as tribal chief. Sarah was.

But . . . just what the hell were they up to?

Longarm's hiding place was still secure, but he felt he had no choice but to abandon it. He rose to his knees and peered over top of the parfleches as the crowd of yelling, yammering Indians raced toward the south end of the encampment.

"Psst!"

"What? Who?"

"Over here, Reverend."

Dascher turned around, his expression puzzled and unhappy. "Who are you?"

"Come here, Reverend. Please." Longarm did not want to emerge from behind the parfleches, out where he might be seen by anyone who turned around. There was no danger if the preacher were seen. After all, the Indians already knew he was there. They had counted on him being there. "Come here, sir."

Dascher moved like a man who was sleepwalking. But he stepped down off the platform and walked stiffly over to Longarm. "What is it, young man? Who are you? What are you doing here? Do you know what has happened with my flock?"

"Sit down, Reverend. Sit on this parfleche, please."

"The what?"

"This rawhide box. Sit on it, please."

"All right. If you wish." Dascher still looked terribly

confused. And quite disappointed that his Mighty Men for Christ had run off without explanation.

"There's something I want you t' do, Reverend. I want you to slip off into the night an' hoof it just as fast as you can go back to Camp Converse."

"Whyever would I do a thing like that, young man?"

"Reverend, I'm a United States deputy marshal, and I hate t' tell you this but I think there is fixing to be some serious trouble here. I want you to get away while you can. Nobody is watching you right now, but if you wait very long they are gonna remember you. And I think things could go awful hard on you when that happens, Reverend. So, please . . . get away from here. Go back to the post an' tell Corporal Lassiter that there's a war brewing out here. He needs to send a dispatch rider to higher headquarters warning them there is gonna be a breakout. Then he needs to fort up and hope a relief column can get there in time to keep the Indians from raising the hair of every one of those few soldiers he's got. D'you understand what I am telling you, Reverend? You need t' go warn the Army about what's going on out here. You can save a lotta lives if you will do that, sir."

"Oh, I believe you are mistaken, son. These men are all Christians now. They have been baptized with the water and with the Spirit. They have been washed clean as new-fallen snow."

"Reverend, I admire you for believin' that. Truly I do. But it won't hurt you none to do as I ask an' it just might save lives."

"My mission is to save souls, Deputy. Yours is to save lives. If you believe the things you have told me, I will not quarrel with you. I will wish you Godspeed as you return to the post to warn those young men and to call for reinforcements. But I cannot do that for you. You see, my place is here. With my flock."

"Reverend, I think your flock has been sheared," Longarm said, pointing toward the south end of the encampment where three score or more of shouting Indian warriors had now cast off their shirts and trousers and were naked, dancing a weaving pattern among newly kindled fires.

And—it was a sight that made Longarm's blood run cold—they were waving repeating lever-action carbines that a greasy trader was handing out as fast as he could snatch them out of crates on the back of his wagon.

Trader, yes. And traitor too. A Frenchman, Longarm saw, judging by his waist-long, tasseled wool cap and scarlet sash. A trader out of French Canada probably.

Longarm felt the fury boil up inside him at the thought of what those repeaters could do in the hands of a wild band of renegades. Whites—blacks and Indians too— would die by the dozens before an uprising of this magnitude could be quelled.

And all for the sake of a few dollars of profit for that French bastard.

There would be time enough to worry about him later, though, Longarm realized. Or else there would be no time at all.

What he had to do right now was to . . . somehow . . . stop a war from happening.

"Pray for me, Reverend," Longarm mumbled out of the corner of his mouth. But when he turned his head toward the spot where Samuel Dascher had just been, all Longarm saw was empty space.

Dascher had left the parfleche he'd been sitting on and was now striding through the firelight toward the dancing, naked savages who he seemed to persist in thinking of as his flock of innocents.

Chapter 34

Longarm jumped to his feet and in a low crouch began running to overtake Samuel Dascher. He did not have any particular plan in mind. He only wanted to reach the man. Tackle him. Talk some sense into him. And get them both out of trouble. Longarm did not pause to think about the consequences if he should be discovered hiding inside the renegade camp.

In fact he needn't have bothered trying to stop Dascher.

The preacher had a long stride and was moving quickly. Worse, he deliberately called attention to himself, shouting and waving his arms and crying out for his "flock" to hear.

"Brothers. You must stop this. Stop!"

And the Indians did stop.

Sarah—Snow Maiden—stopped them with a simple sweep of her arm. The wild ones stopped their yipping and dancing and waited for their leader, their true leader, to make her wishes known.

She said something that Longarm could not understand, her speech brief and stern. For a moment Longarm, crouching there in shadow, thought she might well have been giving the Reverend Dascher an exemption from violence, a reprieve so to speak.

Snow Maiden spoke with conviction, her chin held high and her bearing regal.

She spoke and the Indians responded. A dozen hands reached out to the Reverend Dascher. They hustled him to the back of the wagon where Snow Maiden now stood, surrounded by a horde of savages with brand-new repeating rifles in their fists.

"Children. Children. What are you doing? Why have you departed from the Word?" the old man cried.

Snow Maiden motioned for the French trader to leave, and he obediently stepped down and hunkered beneath the wagon. Not a bad idea, Longarm thought. Out of sight, out of mind.

She motioned again and Many Thumbs leaped onto the tailgate of the wagon to join her. By now almost half of the renegades held torches in addition to their new repeaters. The scene on the tailgate was well lighted. Many Thumbs's necklace of human bone glistened white in the light of the torches.

Sarah spoke. A few curt words. And Samuel Dascher was lifted by a dozen eager pairs of arms, lifted onto the tailgate, where he stood stooped over and cringing.

It was too far away to be sure, but Longarm thought he saw tear tracks glistening on the old man's cheeks. Dascher was crying.

Hell, Longarm didn't blame him.

"Repent," Snow Maiden shouted.

"What?"

"Is that not what you say when you go to this white god of yours?"

"Oh, my dear girl. The Lord is not a white god. He is truly God. To all men. To you and much as to me. To red and well as to white." The old boy was scared out of his wits, but that was not stopping him from his mission. Longarm admired him for that.

Snow Maiden was not listening. She threw her head back and lifted her arms. Toward her gods, Longarm assumed. In a low, flat voice she began to chant, and for some reason Longarm was pleased that he did not know her words.

When she was done chanting, she fixed Samuel Dascher with a searching look that she held for long heartbeats.

Then she turned her back, and the crowd went crazy, screaming and loosing wild, ululating cries. Dancing and stomping and brandishing their rifles and their torches.

Longarm did not know what effect this was having on the Reverend Dascher. The warriors were making so much noise that the reverend's words, whatever they may have been, could not be heard although Longarm could see the man's lips moving.

Perhaps he was praying. It would have been good if he was.

Snow Maiden held her arms up again and instantly the crowd became quiet. She nodded to Many Thumbs, who was standing meekly at her side, and the bloodthirsty war leader snatched a war club from his sash.

Before Longarm could intervene, the club flashed and the stone ball affixed to the striking end of the club came crashing down on the back of Samuel Dascher's skull.

The preacher's eye bulged and soft gray brain matter began to leak out of his head.

The Reverend J. Samuel Dascher was dead before his knees buckled and dropped him onto the tailgate.

Many Thumbs shrieked a bloodcurdling war cry and held his bloodied club high, then kicked Samuel Dascher's lifeless body off the end of the tailgate.

The assembled warriors went crazy with blood lust then, screaming and dancing and firing their rifles into the air.

Longarm felt sick to his stomach.

Chapter 35

Longarm stood there, helpless to vent his fury. He . . . *shit, he was standing there. And he had his Colt in his hand*.

A few of the wildly screaming Indians on the back fringes of the crowd saw him. They stopped what they were doing and stared at him. Some, a few, gave him darkly menacing glares. Most just seemed surprised. Or curious.

When the hell had he stood upright? He hadn't been thinking, merely reacting to the sight of the meek preacher having his brains beat out.

But . . . damn! What a stupid thing to do.

So much for any idea that he might slip away and fetch the Army to put down this movement of evil that Snow Maiden and Many Thumbs were inciting.

More and more of the Indians realized that their companions to the rear had grown silent. Those turned, looked, and also became quiet and still. In another minute or two the whole fucking mob was looking at him, Snow Maiden and Many Thumbs included.

The Colt in Longarm's fist was perfectly capable of killing those two principals standing on the back of the wagon. Those and four others. If he was lucky and could dispatch both Many Thumbs and Snow Maiden cleanly with only two bullets.

But after that. . . .

Shee-it!

Longarm squared his shoulders and held the Colt high so all could see.

"Know this," he shouted over the heads of the mob. "Long Arm says that Many Thumbs is a man without honor. Many Thumbs should wear a dress for he has no balls. Long Arm challenges Many Thumbs to a duel. One against one as it was in the old days. Long Arm will meet Many Thumbs and kill him. This you who watch will see with your own eyes."

Longarm shoved the revolver back into its holster, then turned his head and spit as if disgusted. He braced his legs wide apart and crossed his arms.

Now if only, he was hoping, some of these red sons of bitches spoke enough English to know what just happened here . . .

The silence hung heavy in the flickering torchlight for eight, ten, a dozen heartbeats. Then the mob erupted into a shrieking frenzy.

But they were dancing and leaping around him. No man's hand touched him. No rifle was pointed in his direction nor any club or knife raised against him.

Longarm stood fast, determined not to flinch no matter what these bastards did. Which, as it happened, was nothing except for the threatening noises they were making. Longarm's challenge had been issued. And his courage had been demonstrated.

The next move, whatever it was, would be up to Many Thumbs. And to Snow Maiden, who seemed to be pulling the warrior chieftain's strings.

Chapter 36

"Kill the white man," Many Thumbs shouted, and a great cry went up among the warriors.

Longarm found it interesting—and under other circumstances might even have found it amusing—that Many Thumbs gave the order in English.

But then he undoubtedly wanted Longarm to know and to be stricken immobile with fear.

"Coward!" Longarm shouted back. "You are a coward afraid to face one lone white man. You boast, Many Thumbs, but I have not seen you kill. I only know you to order others to kill. You have no stomach to face a man yourself. I spit on you, Many Thumbs. You are a woman."

He turned his head and spit. Actually, he was pretty damn proud of himself that he could muster up the saliva to get anything out.

"Coward!" he taunted again.

Many Thumbs swelled up with wounded pride. He looked like he was going to come apart at the joints and explode into a thousand pieces. The war leader shouted something in his own tongue, something that Longarm was just as happy not knowing, and the mob again went wild.

But this time none of them threatened Longarm with their weapons. It seemed quite an improvement.

"You would fight?" Many Thumbs yelled from the back of the freight wagon.

"I would fight," Longarm agreed boldly.

"How you fight, Long Arm?"

"One on one," Longarm returned. "With hands or knives or guns, however you wish. I will fight you, Many Thumbs. I will kill you. I will take your head back to the fort with me for all to see." He did not know where that taunt had come from, but he'd said it and he would by God do it. If he was alive at the end of this fight, that is. There seemed a strong possibility that he might not be, considering how damn many crazed Indians there were here.

"I will break your back and have your balls cooked in a stew," Many Thumbs yelled.

"Eating the balls of real men is the only way you could ever have any, woman," Longarm yelled back. "Go put on a dress. Maybe some man will take pity on you and fuck you in the ass."

Many Thumbs gnashed his teeth and began to tremble from his great fury. That was one thoroughly pissed-off Indian, Longarm thought.

With a roar and a lunge, Many Thumbs threw himself off the wagon tailgate and came racing through the crowd, which parted to give him way. The mob reassembled in a tight circle with Many Thumbs and Custis Long in the center.

Many Thumbs came on with blood in his eye and murder in whatever he had where a heart should have been.

Chapter 37

Many Thumbs barked out an order, and a moment later one of the warriors produced a rawhide thong perhaps a half-inch wide and eight feet or so in length. Many Thumbs thrust out his left wrist, his hate-filled eyes boring into Longarm's while a warrior quickly tied one end of the thong around Many Thumbs's wrist.

Understanding now the way this fight would take place, Longarm grunted. And stepped forward. He offered his left arm to the warrior with the rawhide, and was secured to Many Thumbs with a gap of roughly five feet between them.

Many Thumbs drew his knife, one of the large trade knives in the Arkansas pattern with a wedge-shaped point and both edges sharpened.

"You die, white man," Many Thumbs snarled.

"Yes, but not today," Longarm answered, taking out his own much smaller belt knife. His was more camp and field tool than weapon, with a single sharp edge and very small guard.

Many Thumbs held his knife high, about shoulder height, with his elbow pointed into the air and his torso leaning back while the two men stayed at the limits of the tether and slowly circled round and round, poised, watching, each waiting for the other to make a move.

Longarm held his weapon at waist level, haft balanced on his palm rather than clutched tightly in his fist as Many Thumbs was doing with his bigger, heavier knife.

"Huh!" Many Thumbs grunted, at the same time stamping his left foot.

Longarm did not react, just continued the slow circling.

"Huh. Huh." This time Many Thumbs advanced a step, then faded back again.

Longarm thought he saw something in Many Thumbs's eyes. Something deadly. A smirk that failed to reach his stoic expression. Longarm braced himself.

Many Thumbs sprang backward, jerking Longarm's left arm with the rawhide. Longarm was ready for him and pulled back, refusing to be yanked forward onto the point of Many Thumbs's knife.

The two resumed their circling.

Longarm noticed rather dimly that there was a roaring that seemed to surround and to hold them. It was the noise of the shrieking, yammering crowd. Longarm paid it no mind. He could feel the pressure of the noise more than hear it, like being immersed deep underwater. The sound itself seemed almost distant, a physical presence that pressed in on him from all sides.

"Huh!" Many Thumbs yanked on the rawhide again. Again Longarm resisted, bracing his legs and pulling back against Many Thumbs's weight.

Many Thumbs apparently wanted to pull Longarm into range of his blade. In order to do that he needed to catch

Longarm with one foot off the ground so as to reduce his balance. He also needed to overpower the white man.

Sweat glistened on Many Thumbs's naked upper body, streaks of moisture gleaming in the torchlight. He wore no war paint, but there was a cruel set to his jaw and arrogance in his facial expression.

He had killed one white man this night. He wanted the blood of another.

Longarm circled. Waited. When the killing moment came, it would be sudden and it would be over in an instant, Longarm knew. This sort of fight cannot drag out.

He had heard that the legendary Louisianan Jim Bowie was a master of this sort of fighting. Except Bowie liked to do it in pitch darkness. That, Longarm thought, was a man with balls.

Many Thumbs's muscles tensed. He was going to try again to yank Longarm onto his blade, Longarm thought.

Except this time . . .

A hint of a smile flickered across Longarm's face. Enough for the big Indian to see.

And when Many Thumbs pulled, Longarm leaped.

Leaped *toward* his enemy, not backward the way Many Thumbs seemed to expect.

Longarm's left hand closed on Many Thumbs's right wrist, clamping down hard and immobilizing the big man's knife. At the same time Longarm's blade flashed low.

Into Many Thumbs's unprotected belly.

Longarm drove the blade deep, twisted it slightly, and yanked upward, ripping through flesh and muscle.

Many Thumbs's eyes went wide and his mouth gaped open.

The two were nose to nose now. Longarm could

smell Many Thumbs's breath and feel his sweat as the two collided.

Many Thumbs gasped. He stumbled backward and stared down at a coil of slippery pink and white gut that was tumbling out of his belly.

The warrior screamed, more in shock and anguish than in actual pain, Longarm thought.

He went to his knees.

Playing to the crowd, Longarm slashed with his knife again, this time severing the rawhide cord.

Many Thumbs toppled onto his side. Acting with swift disdain, Longarm straddled the still-living warrior, picked up the man's own Arkansas knife, and used the heavy blade to hack Many Thumbs's head loose from his shoulders.

When he was done, Longarm straightened to his full height and thrust his arm aloft with Many Thumbs's head clutched in his fist by the hair.

The mob of Indians became silent, all their cheering and shrieking muted by the shocking fact that their leading warrior not only had been killed, but had been mutilated as well.

Longarm brandished the head at them and they backed quietly away and began melting into the darkness, dropping their torches as they went, as if they were ashamed to be seen in the firelight, until only Longarm, Snow Maiden, and the trembling Frenchman were left.

"You killed those people back at the post, didn't you?" Longarm accused.

Snow Maiden had no remorse in her haughty expression, only regret that her plan had not worked. She held her head high and proud. "The guns were due to arrive soon. I had to stop you from coming here," she said.

"You even made that girl kill herself."

"Of course."

"And Lieutenant Haynes? He was in love with you, you know."

"He was a pig. White pig." She turned her head and spit to emphasize her feelings about white men in general and George Haynes in particular.

"You spread your legs for this white pig," Longarm said.

"Your touch made me sick."

Longarm laughed. "You lying little bitch, you enjoyed it every bit as much as I did. I have to admit that you're a pretty good fuck, Sarah."

"I am Snow Maiden."

"You're a prisoner of the United States Government is what you are, Sarah, and if they don't hang you . . . which they damn sure might . . . at the very least you won't never walk this land as a free woman. Count on that, you miserable piece of shit."

Snow Maiden gasped. Her hands went to her throat and her expression was bleak. "You would not. I am priest to my people. This Great Father of yours says all peoples can worship how they please. You cannot take me away from them."

"You don't know as much as you think you do, bitch. Now turn around. Your parishioners are fixing to see you with manacles on your wrists."

Sarah obediently turned. And then spun back around with a small, nickel-plated revolver in her fist.

Longarm hadn't known what she would attempt, but he'd been certain she would not acquiesce that easily. He was ready for her. So was his Colt.

Before Snow Maiden could shoot, a .44-caliber slug impacted square on her forehead. It snapped her head backward, and the back of her head exploded in a spray of blood and brain and bone.

"Bitch!" Longarm muttered after glancing toward the limp, deflated body of the Reverend Samuel Dascher.

"You," Longarm snapped toward the cowering Frenchman. "Crawl out from under that wagon an' start cleaning up this mess. I reckon you're responsible for it, so you can start loading bodies t' take back to what passes for civilization out here."

Longarm glared down at the dead, then stalked away to go fetch his horse—well, some Indian's horse actually—from the trees.

Most likely, he thought, all those would-be renegades would get back to Camp Converse ahead of him.

That was fine. He was in no hurry now except to get the hell home to Denver for some of that relaxation and easy living that Billy Vail kept promising him.

Watch for

**LONGARM AND THE
OWLHOOTS' GRAVEYARD**

the 332nd novel in the exciting LONGARM
series from Jove

Coming in July!

Explore the exciting Old West with one of the men who made it wild!

LONGARM AND THE TALKING SPIRIT #305	0-515-13716-2
LONGARM AND THE MONTANA MADMEN #308	0-515-13774-X
LONGARM SETS THE STAGE #310	0-515-13813-4
LONGARM AND THE DEVIL'S BRIDE #311	0-515-13836-3
LONGARM AND THE TWO-BIT POSSE #312	0-515-13853-3
LONGARM AND THE COMSTOCK LODE KILLERS #314	
	0-515-13877-0
LONGARM AND THE LOST PATROL #315	0-515-13888-6
LONGARM AND THE UNWELCOME WOOLIES #316	
	0-515-13900-9
LONGARM AND THE PAIUTE INDIAN WAR #317	0-515-13934-3
LONGARM AND THE LUNATIC #318	0-515-13944-0
LONGARM AND THE SIDEKICK FROM HELL #319	0-515-13956-4
LONGARM AND THE TEXAS TREASURE HUNT #320	
	0-515-13966-1
LONGARM AND THE LITTLE LADY #321	0-515-13987-4
LONGARM AND THE MISSING MISTRESS #322	
	0-515-14011-2
LONGARM AND THE SCARLET RIDER #323	0-515-14019-8
LONGARM AND KILGORE'S REVENGE #324	0-515-14030-9
LONGARM AND A HORSE OF A DIFFERENT COLOR #325	
	0-515-14043-0
LONGARM AND THE BAD BREAK #326	0-515-14055-4
LONGARM AND THE UNGRATEFUL GUN #327	0-515-14069-4
LONGARM AND THE RAILROAD MURDERS #328	0-515-14091-0
LONGARM AND THE RESTLESS REDHEAD #329	0-515-14122-4
LONGARM AND THE APACHE WAR #330	0-515-14130-5

**AVAILABLE WHEREVER BOOKS ARE SOLD OR AT
PENGUIN.COM**

(Ad # B112)

**GIANT-SIZED ADVENTURE FROM
AVENGING ANGEL LONGARM.**

LONGARM AND THE UNDERCOVER MOUNTIE
0-515-14017-1

**THIS ALL-NEW, GIANT-SIZED ADVENTURE IN THE
POPULAR ALL-ACTION SERIES PUTS THE "WILD"
BACK IN THE WILD WEST.**

**U.S. MARSHAL CUSTIS LONG AND ROYAL CANADIAN
MOUNTIE SEARGEANT FOSTER HAVE AN EVIL TOWN
TO CLEAN UP—WHERE OUTLAWS INDULGE THEIR
WICKED WAYS. BUT FIRST, THEY'LL HAVE TO STAY
AHEAD OF THE MEANEST VIGILANTE COMMITTEE
ANYBODY EVER RAN FROM.**

**AVAILABLE WHEREVER BOOKS ARE SOLD OR AT
PENGUIN.COM**

JAKE LOGAN
TODAY'S HOTTEST ACTION WESTERN!

☐ SLOCUM AND THE BAD-NEWS BROTHERS #302

        0-515-13715-4

☐ SLOCUM AND THE ORPHAN EXPRESS #303   0-515-13733-2

☐ SLOCUM AND THE LADY REPORTER #304   0-515-13750-2

☐ SLOCUM AT WHISKEY LAKE #305   0-515-13773-1

☐ SLOCUM AND THE REBEL YELL #306   0-515-13794-4

☐ SLOCUM AND THE SHERIFF OF GUADALUPE #307

        0-515-13812-6

☐ SLOCUM AND THE HANGMAN'S LADY #308   0-515-13835-5

☐ SLOCUM AND THE CROOKED SHERIFF #309   0-515-13852-5

☐ SLOCUM AND THE TETON TEMPTRESS #310   0-515-13876-2

☐ SLOCUM AND AND THE SLANDERER #311   0-515-13876-2

☐ SLOCUM AND THE BIXBY BATTLE #312   0-515-13887-8

☐ SLOCUM AND THE RUNAWAY BRIDE #313   0-515-13899-1

☐ SLOCUM AND THE DEADWOOD DEAL #314   0-515-13933-5

☐ SLOCUM'S GOLD MOUNTAIN #315   0-515-13943-2

☐ SLOCUM'S SWEET REVENGE #316   0-515-13955-6

☐ SLOCUM AND THE SIERRE MADRAS GOLD #317   0-515-13965-3

☐ SLOCUM AND THE PRESIDIO PHANTOMS #318   0-515-13986-6

☐ SLOCUM AND LADY DEATH #319   0-515-14010-4

☐ SLOCUM AND THE SULFUR VALLEY WIDOWS #320

        0-515-14018-X

☐ SLOCUM AND THE VANISHED #321   0-515-13684-0

☐ SLOCUM AND THE WATER WITCH #322   0-515-14042-2

☐ SLOCUM AND THE MOJAVE GUNS #323   0-515-14054-6

☐ SLOCUM AND THE TWO GOLD BULLETS #324   0-515-14068-6

☐ SLOCUM AND THE BOSS'S WIFE #325   0-515-14090-2

☐ SLOCUM AND THE BIG PAYBACK #326   0-515-14121-6

☐ SLOCUM AND THE MESCAL SMUGGLERS #327   0-515-14129-1

AVAILABLE WHEREVER BOOKS ARE SOLD OR AT
PENGUIN.COM

(Ad # B110)